Dreams of
Eli

VAN HEERLING

CONTENTS

ALSO by VAN HEERLING

Malaika

"This is by far the best piece of literature, under full novel length, I have EVER read..."

~ T.M Souders

For my father.

Always.

ACKNOWLEDGMENT

To my wife, thank you for keeping me grounded and for your patience. I'll figure it out one day.

And to Matthew, thank you for making me a better storyteller. I am trying to live up to your impossible standard.

And finally, to you grasping this ebook or paperback within your hands. I used to think I wrote for myself; what a foolish thought. This story is for you and your loved ones.

NOTE FROM THE AUTHOR

Below are a few words and phrases of the day that the reader may or may not know.

Boiled shirt - popular slang for a clean shirt.

California collar - hangman's noose.

Expressman: one who delivered mail, packages, and parcels; a mailman.

Inexpressibles: prudish name given to trousers or pants to avoid being vulgar in speech, from the first half of the century. Also known as sit-down-upons, unmentionables and unwhisperables.

Pull foot: to leave in a hurry.

Some Pumpkins: someone or something impressive.

Reference: *The Writer's Guide to Everyday Life in the 1800s* by Marc McCutcheon

At the precipice of death, more often than not, we think of the ones we love, the friendships we are about to lose, the fights we wish we did not win, and the missed opportunities to forgive. Some say that sorrow, regret, and empathy in man are reasons to believe man may be worthy of salvation.

I hope so.

~ **VH**

DREAMS of ELI

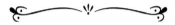

May 1863
Eli, Age 26

During a skirmish two days ago, while in retreat, I lost my company. Somewhere in the backwoods of Northern Mississippi I finish a piece of stale bread, stand up, and lay my rifle against my shoulder.

It is not the crack of the enemy Enfield rifle round that startles me. It is the sifting whispers of the bullet as it splits the wild grass in my direction. The shooter, by the sound of it, is between four hundred and five hundred yards off. I know this because I have the same standard issue. The ball strikes me hard in the lower left shin. White searing pain shreds up my leg and body like a thunderbolt.

I stumble. My rifle catches most of my weight as I plow it into the soft earth from where I had just risen. But the shock is too great. I lose my grip—falling hard and fast to the cool soil where I crush my face against a large granite

1

boulder. The flavors of shattered teeth and metallic blood sour my mouth. But all I can think about is the next eighteen seconds—enough time for my enemy to reload. The shot that I will never hear is upon me. I knew I would die in these woods. I just did not realize I would be alone. But at this end I do not want my brothers next to me. I want Cora. I wait for the final shot, but it never comes. Instead, blackness takes me.

CHAPTER ONE

May 1863
Eli, Age 26

I hear nothing but ringing in my head. My legs and rump scrape against the ground at half a trot. A man is dragging me—to where I do not know. Feebly, I mumble something. My captor slows for a moment. He crouches over me for a listen, and then continues on. The daylight is unbearably heavy as my eyelids collapse. I fall back into oblivion.

April 1846
Eli, Age 9

The first time I see her I am fishing with Ezra, an orphan Negro boy that is my best friend. I will never forget the moment I hear that twig break—those eyes. We both turn. Ezra says that he saw her first. To this day I do not know if he is right, but I do know I am forever changed. She comes out from behind a magnolia tree. I think she has been there awhile. We both stand as she bashfully makes her way down the hill to the edge of the water where our poles lay on the bank.

"You are that Negro boy-doctor, are you not?" she says, pointing to Ezra.

"I suppose I am. Ezra Johnson," he says, extending his hand. Ezra had been adopted by Mister Johnson, the town physician. He became the doctor's apprentice nearly two years ago. Already he is adept at bloodletting, lancing, and various herbal fever-breaking concoctions.

"You boys ready for a swim?" We are, however, she is not, seemingly. She wears a tattered off-white Sunday dress with no shoes. Before I know it though, both her bashfulness and her dress flop to the sand and a splash douses our faces. "Come on, the water is wonderful!" I have never swum with a girl before. I mean, not with one wearing only her unmentionables. For a nine-year-old boy I do not know what to do with myself.

Ezra stays at the bank. He never has liked to swim beyond the shallows. I have yet to ride him about this. I think it may have something to do with his parents.

"How come you have not asked my name?" I query, as I swim to her.

She smiles and spits water in my face. She laughs, "Because I already know your name. I know all about you, Eli." I am puzzled. "I know that you were born here and that you fish every Sunday."

"Really? What else do you know?"

"That you have been looking for a girl like me."

I blush. "How is that?"

"Word around town is you need help with the numbers. And I have been looking for something too."

"Really? What?"

"A boy like you . . . you know, a challenge."

"She rightly has you pegged, Eli," Ezra concedes.

"Are you some kind of math genius?" I ask.

She presses her lips into a wry smile. I am not sure how to respond to this, but I like it. As she swims away from me, her legs brush against me. A rush of something too good not to be a sin flutters through me. I am not totally sure what it is, but I know it came from her, and I want as much of it as possible.

She is not shy as she pulls herself from the water and onto the bank. Her bottoms are sheer and the water races down her slim body. I should turn away, but I cannot. So I stare at her as she slips her dress on, fighting with it as it sticks against her shimmering skin.

"I will see you, Eli." Her eyes reflect the blue sky. I gaze toward her, besotted.

"Wait!" I say. "When will I see you? What is your name?"

She giggles as she delicately negotiates the hill and turns back to me.

"Tonight is lesson one. My name is Cora. Cora Samantha

Hannah." She disappears into the trees.

"Ezra," I say, "never in my life have I wanted to learn arithmetic more than in this moment."

CHAPTER TWO

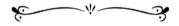

June 1854
Eli, Age 17

At eighteen, Ezra's physique rivals most men. I no longer worry for him like I did when we were boys. For years Mister Johnson has been whipping him. And for nearly the same amount of time Ezra has been enduring other unpleasantries.

It is on this night that Mister Johnson is going to meet his maker. And in a most gruesome of ways.

Wails of agonizing pain, although muffled, have been coming from Mister Johnson's home all evening. Townsfolk think nothing of the wailings—just another Negro boy enduring his nightly discipline.

None seem to realize it is Mister Johnson who cries. Ezra has cinched his master's hands behind his back. They are bound with the rope that had once held Ezra captive as a boy, long ago stained with his blood.

DREAMS OF ELI

Sickly snapping sounds harmonize with futile screams. And slave or master—all flesh separates under the whip.

I wish I could say Ezra's vengeance stops after scores of lashings, but it does not. He snaps the handle off his broom, fashioning a splintered club of sorts. He then violates Mister Johnson with the broom handle for hours, long after the doctor's viscera have been splayed.

Few knew of Mister Johnson's insatiable appetite for sodomy, but Ezra and I knew well. In the past, such abuse had not been something Ezra was willing to speak about, but the clues were there to be discovered.

Ezra is eleven when I coerce it out of him.

"Promise me, Eli," he says frantically one day while at the lake, "promise me you will not tell a soul. He will end me." He says this following a particularly difficult evening with the doctor. The water turns pink around Ezra. He nervously splashes me and swims away from the area, hoping I had not noticed.

It does not matter that we are the best of friends. This secret is one never to be spoken of again. It seems stronger than even our bond. In my gut I know that I should tell someone. It is not right, but who will listen?

After the broom handle, Ezra ropes him around the main beam of the home. Instead of hanging him by his neck, Ezra hangs him by his feet, like swine.

He retrieves a surgical tool from the doctor's satchel. The art of precision makes for short work. I have not known Ezra to be overly religious, but I cannot help but think that the thoroughness of such bloodletting is an exorcism of sorts.

Ezra leaves town before anyone figures out what has happened. I believe he may have been planning this day for years. I do not wish him ill for not telling me. I am grateful that he did not. I just wish he could have given me a proper farewell. I miss him.

Of course, if he is ever again spotted in the state of Mississippi, his homecoming will be met with the wrong end of a rope and the steady sway of a Southern bough.

CHAPTER THREE

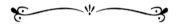

May 1863
Eli, Age 26

Tiny clinking sounds pull me from my uncon-
sciousness. The scent of earth is thick within my
nostrils, and my vision is blurry. Hazy, golden
light showers my surroundings, as pungent kerosene smoke
fills my chest. To my left I feel the warm glow of embers.

The clinking continues as a figure moves about three
paces in front of me. A figure I did not realize was there
until now. The fabric, a deep blue, hangs from his shoulders
— Union.

I am in hell. The burning in my leg is constant, like the
heat of the glowing embers, but I will not surrender to the
pain. I lie on the rock floor with only a thin blanket under
me. My hands are tied upon my lap; my legs however are
untethered. A sipping sound meets my ear, and then the tap
of a metal spoon thuds on a wooden surface. The scent is
unmistakable—Mississippi gumbo.

I swoon at the thought of a belly full of gumbo. For weeks I have not had a decent meal. I must have moaned, because the figure turns quickly. I see an indefinite mush. A raspy, thick voice booms.

"No, no no no," he says as he kneels down next to me. Is this a friend? Liquid is being poured to my right. I still cannot see him. "I will tell you when you may wake up. We have much to discuss. And it will be painful." I do not know what to make of these words. His breath hits me . . . a white cloth smothers my face. The pressure of the hand concentrates over my nose and mouth. I breathe deeply, inhaling chloroform. And he does it with gumbo on his breath.

February 1854
Eli, Age 17

Of my memories of Cora, few are more treasured than of us necking under starry nights. Such nights are, of course, and fittingly so, some of the most painful to relive. Dear God, I miss her.

"Do you care for some of my chocolate?" she whispers in my ear, as if keeping a secret from the night sky. Mister Hannah has recently come back from Massachusetts. Cora tells me a favorite pastime of her father is to discover decadent chocolates. Anything for his Sam. Everyone calls her Sam.

It was not until she met me at the lake that she, on a whim, decided to choose the one person in her life she would allow to call her by her first true name. I like being different.

Her finger presses against my tongue as chocolate dances across my mouth. Gently she replaces her finger with a short soft kiss.

"How is that?" she asks as she pulls away from me.

"Scrumptious," I say as her eyes penetrate deep into mine. In this moment I want to pledge my life to her. She makes love to me on this chilly February night. For me, the earth shifts beneath us, and the stars above do not turn their gaze.

CHAPTER FOUR

May 1863
Eli, Age 26

I feel my body teetering to the right. Pressure against my wrists holds me in place. I am sitting. My wrists are tied behind a high-backed chair. My eyelids feel like sandpaper as they rise, scraping against my eyes. I still am unable to see. Something covers them. Linen. I reach to uncover the obstruction, having forgotten my wrists are held fast. The chloroform still lingers on my hot, dry breath. The pain in my left leg blazes, but it is different than before. I try to move my legs but they too have been bound.

I mumble incoherently. If not for the chair, I surely would fall on my face again. To my left I feel the fire from before. Only it is stronger now as it spits and crackles. It sounds like something iron prods it. I shudder at the idea of red-hot iron blistering my skin.

"Why," I mumble weakly, not knowing if I am heard. Footsteps crush bits of sand as I feel my host place a hand upon the back of the chair. A warm hand rests against my shoulder. My head still slumps forward right. Gently the hand releases from my shoulder and lifts my chin upward so that I may face him. I moan again. My jaw feels like it is broken. Instantly, a flash memory of my face smashing against the granite boulder hits my mind. A deep groan escapes from the belly of my "friend." No doubt his face is mere inches from mine.

If I had any strength whatever, I would fight or struggle, even crawl for my freedom. I feel the linen peeling back to where he rests it atop my head. I raise my eyelids, but just barely. A splash of light penetrates my sight as he peels my eyes open. I see only whiteness, and recoil in pain. Just as I am beginning to see the etching of a figure coming, he pulls the material back over my face.

"You are not ready to see. Besides, you will not want to see this," he says. The footsteps return to the fire. I hear the familiar scrape of iron being pulled from embers, followed by sizzles and spits as it is doused with what I suppose is water.

My sudden cries pull me to consciousness. I recognize the sweet, sickly taste of chloroform in my mouth tongue and throat.

I open my eyes to blackness. A moment later, my head is being shoved against the chair back. He forces my mouth open. I fight to breathe as I feel the crunch of a molar being uprooted along the top right side of my mouth. The taste of hot blood overwhelms me. He withdraws the contraption from my mouth and with several tiny "tinks," pieces of my tooth fall against a pan. A grating scrape of metal against metal scratches at my eardrums as he sets his extraction tool aside.

"Are you going to tell me?" he says, almost cheerfully, as if we have been in a delightful midsummer afternoon conversation. I try to speak. Perhaps I can mutter a word or two. Had I been speaking to him while under his chloroform spell?

"Cora," I mumble.

"Yes, tell me more about Cora."

"Cora!?" I struggle. I feel five concentrated points push my chest—his fingertips pin me and my feeble and hopeless aggression against the chair. Had I confessed her name? "Stay away from her," I manage to slur, as shards of splintered teeth sputter from my lips. I doubt that he could understand me, but my intensity seems to carry the message.

I wish that I could *see* this oppressor! What does he want? I hear a hardy, placating laugh. My body may be weak and my mind adrift, but I still know who I am. I have never *wanted* to kill a man, until this moment.

Truthfully, within the recesses of my mind I know that whatever was confessed of Cora really does not matter. No man could touch her, no man could hurt her. Not even me.

I hear the familiar suck of a weathered cork popping from a bottle. A waft of whiskey burns my nose as my head is pressed against the chair back. The liquor pours generously into my aching mouth. My head slumps forward, spilling the contents down my chest. The vapors choke me, and I begin to hack. I am shirtless, and my pants are unbuttoned. My mouth pulses in tandem with my heaving lungs as I try to breathe. As my tongue instinctively rolls over my gums, I discover that the three rear molars have been removed along the upper right side. Had I not answered him correctly? I curl my fingers into my palms, hoping they will not be next.

I am infantry. What do I know? What could he possibly want with me? Perhaps he was aiming to extract my company's strategy or short-term plans? Fearing this to be the case, I press what is left of my chow mashers against each other, praying this is not the last time they meet. I never before appreciated them. Now with the prospect of the rest of them being ripped away, I suddenly find myself quite fond of them.

Again my head hits the chair back as his hand covers my nose with the poison cloth. I breathe in as the iron is lifted off the table and clasps around a remaining molar.

"This is going to hurt," he says. I whimper. My gums tear as the unforgiving clamp rips out yet another tooth. The pain then lessens, as the poison fades me away. But as the blackness falls upon me, I think of Ezra and this war. He would not be proud of me, fighting for the wrong side. Fighting for the ways of my father's generation, rather than what I know.

My consciousness continues to fade into the silence as the drone of my captor's baritone voice disappears within my mind.

CHAPTER FIVE

March 1856
Eli, Age 19

Monday, March 3rd, 1856, I sit on the porch steps of my father's home with my head on my lap. It is raining gently. I hear the splash of wet footsteps as a man clears his throat and touches my shoulder. I hoped that the rain would have washed my tears from my face, as my eyes meet my visitor, but not so.

"Son, you all right?"

I wipe my face.

"Yes," I say unconvincingly, with flushed cheeks and rubbed raw eyes. The man, an expressman, rummages through a leather bag strapped across his chest. His wool hat is no match for a sudden burst of heavy rain falling. I am much relieved to see that he is not the same expressman Cora and I had the pleasure of meeting a little more than a year ago. Had he been, I do not believe I would be so held together.

"Ahh," he continues, "I am looking for Eli West."

I nod. The letter is bound in twine and dated September 17th, 1855, from California. I reach in my pocket, but find only lint.

"What do I owe for the trouble, sir?" I say, as I turn away and head for the door.

"No need, son. This letter is marked for home delivery and has been paid in full. Please accept my apologies. It is quite late. Indeed, looks like the better part of six months since it was placed in our charge . . . been in my keep these last couple weeks. It was sent from California; should have been at your doorstep within twenty-four days. Although I confess, twenty-four days is a rarity." I nod, gesturing that I am grateful for its arrival nonetheless.

He tips his hat toward me with a hesitant smile. It seems he wants to impart a kindness or sympathy, but at the last moment he turns away and departs.

I retreat to the porch and sit in my father's rocking chair. Instead of unraveling the twine, I pull it over the corners of the parcel. My fingers are cold and ache all over. Stuffed tightly within a securely folded paper cover are five separate trifolds of paper. Instantly I recognize the steady handwriting. This June would mark two years since Ezra fled.

Dear Eli,

My dear friend. I am not certain how you will receive this letter.

Whether you will accept it or cast it aside. If the latter, I do not blame you. I am sorry that I did not come to see you that ill-fated June night. I was distraught and felt I could not trust anyone. Not Samantha or even you.

I concede to the reports in the papers. Their account was mostly right. But, of course, they did not know my motives. I had to make sure he suffered for the injustices done not only to me, but to many others . . . I will not write of my justifications. What is done is done.

I do confess, I fear I have fated my soul to Hell. Taking another's life changed me. I am a different man.

I am sure you have noted that this letter is postmarked: California. Please do not attempt to write. I will be well into The Territory once you are in receipt of these words. This, in all likelihood, will be the only letter you receive from me.

He continues page over page about less than virtuous women in the gold country, brawls, and a card game that ended in a rope burn around his neck and a stolen horse.

In closing, please give my love and good tidings to Sam. I suppose you have been married for a year by now and may have a little one, or perhaps one on the way? Truly I hope this is a blessing in your life. I am sorry I have missed these last couple years.

A tear drops onto the letter as I continue to read. If only he knew what he had missed.

P.S.

I met a scratcher in San Francisco—went by the name of Lucky Fingers. I tried to convince him that his doctored banknotes successfully passing from hand to hand in California was about as likely as a colored dining alone with his master's wife. But Lucky thought otherwise. Two weeks later I was a witness along with a hundred others to his hanging. He could not see me within the multitude, but his last words before his wet eyes met the executioner's black hood were "Ezra, my friend, you knew." He seemed a right likeable guy, if you looked past his crookin'. One night in a card game, I won some gold from him. He tried to plank up with his "paper," but I insisted on the gold.

I sift through the trifolds finding nothing, but then I smile as I tip the folded cover into my hand. Out falls a small piece of sparkling yellow metal.

CHAPTER SIX

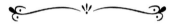

May 1863
Eli, Age 26

I wake to something pinching my big toe. I try to pull my leg away from the pain, but a hand holds it fast. I manage to roll part of the gauze off my right eye as I rub my face against the blankets. I am dizzy as the light blazes against my once-covered eye.

He has yet to notice I am fully awake. I assume he is used to me moving in my sleep. I hear him pull something metal from a bag as it rattles against other metal objects.

He cups my foot within one of his palms while his other hand positions the metal against my big toe. I feel its coldness press just below the nail above the digit. Fire erupts as he glides the metal deep into the skin, scraping bone.

"AAHHHHHHHHHH!"

The blade drops as he rushes toward me. His hands, wet with blood, pull the linen back over my eye. I try to rip my hands from their binds, but there is no strength in me. The pain of my toe settles as chloroform again infiltrates my lungs.

August 1854
Eli, Age 17

Quietly, as this day's end nears, I wait in the Hannah family room lighted by half a dozen lavender-scented candles. I suppress a mild cough as my lungs object to the potent waxy air. Before she retreated to her room, Missus Hannah had been kind enough to let me in, but had asked I not stay too long.

Emily, Cora's ten-year-old sister, is amid a particularly wicked round of coughing from consumption. I risk exposure, but I have found it increasingly difficult being away from Cora.

I am not allowed in Emily's room. I pray she will pull through, but after six months the doctor says the sickness has not shown sign of attenuation.

This illness seems to be the same one Mister Hannah was subjected to last February during his travels to Massachusetts, but from which he had recovered. Overcome with guilt, he has forbidden himself from even laying his eyes upon his youngest, so fearful that further sickness will befall her. Perhaps in his good intentions he deprives her of what she needs most.

Cora walks into the hall from her mother's room and stops with a bottle in her hand. She studies it, and then pushes Emily's door. I do not believe she knows that I am her audience. Emily's room is lighted by a single candle. Cora leaves the door slightly open and sets the bottle atop an ornate nightstand. She places her hand on the sick child's forehead, and I watch as Cora's shoulders slump forward. A spell of disenchantment seems to befall her as she pulls her sister's covers close to her chin.

Cora retrieves a spoon from her apron and uncorks the bottle, carefully pouring a syrupy tonic into the basin and then spooning the medicine into the child's mouth.

"Just one more after this one, Em."

Her sister shakes her head violently. "It hurts," she croaks, as she pulls the covers over her mouth. Cora adjusts the blankets again and sits next to Emily.

"I need you to be strong for me, Em. Just one more spoonful."

"Why?" she asks.

"Because, the doctor said—"

"But it is not working. Nothing works. I just keep getting—and I . . ." Her gaze moves to the flame of the candle.

"It will work. Now open up. And think good thoughts. Good thoughts." Emily swallows another spoonful, then devilishly smiles at her big sister.

"Now, what is this about?" Cora asks.

"Are you going to marry Eli?"

"See, you are feeling better."

"Maybe. Well, are you?"

"Little sis! Are you sweet on my Eli?"

"If he asked me . . . I might say yes," Emily bashfully whispers.

"Well, tell you what, when you get better we will both woo him, and may the best *wooer* win. Deal?"

Emily nods.

"You know he has been watching us this whole time." Emily tilts her head, peeking over Cora's shoulder, stripping me of my anonymity. Cora turns toward me with flushing cheeks. I hear a hoarse giggle, and then an abrupt burst of whooping cough. I am alarmed. Cora casually reaches across the bed, snatching up several handkerchiefs, and holds them against Emily's mouth. The coughs muffle against the material, and after a moment Cora quietly closes the door.

I feel I have intruded. I step out onto the porch, and a couple minutes later Cora joins me. Clumped in her hand are Emily's soiled handkerchiefs.

In a pail of water by the porch railing, she dunks the handkerchiefs, twisting and bunching them until the water is a foggy pink. Horrified, I step back. Cora stifles tears as she turns and walks away from me.

"I know that you want to help us, but please go home. I need to be with my sister." She suddenly breaks down into sobs as she falls to her knees. Restraining my urge to hold her, I respectfully stand still and let her weep. Weep for a sister possibly not long for this world.

As I walk home I look to the twilight sky and wonder — with all of God's grace in the world, why must the living endure such sorrows.

CHAPTER SEVEN

May 1863
Eli, Age 26

I wake with a start. As I shiver far from the fire glow, it mocks me with its warmth. For a moment the amber firelight dazzles me as I realize I can see. The linen must have fallen away. My mouth is foul with whiskey. In my fog I do not remember drinking it. A pained moaning sound nearby hurts my ears. As I come to, the moaning becomes unbearably loud. It is me!

"Shhh!" I hear, but I do not see anyone.

"Ahhhhhh!" I bellow as I try to muster my wits.

"Shut up!" is barked in my direction, but I cannot help myself. My mouth is painfully stuffed with something along the upper right side.

"Ahhhhhhhh!" I scream again. This time I am even more coherent and aware. I hear a shuffling and a pair of feet stomp. A dark fist suddenly swings down toward me. I block it with my face. Knuckles pop in the fiery amber-darkness, or perhaps it is the cracking of my neck as my head hits the dirt. I am dizzy again. I feel the weight of a blanket cover my body as the night takes me back.

September 1854
Eli, Age 17

The soles of my shoes press into the muddy earth as I collect wildflowers. Lord knows what blossoms comprise my growing bouquet. All I know is that they are colorful, and their scent speaks for me and my sentiments.

I stomp my feet against the first step of Cora's porch, shedding most of the mud from my boots. I stand at the doorway with my makeshift bouquet in hand. These flowers now seem more like a sloppy bunch of weeds, clumsily grasped. I knock, hoping it is not too soon. But I know that it *is* too soon.

Slowly the oak door opens, and Cora stands in front of me, exposing herself to the weather and a fool of a boy holding a gesture of love. I feel a whoosh of warmth press against my face as the heat escapes her home. I do not smile. I do not step forward. I stay put, drenching wet, hair matted, and silent.

Cora's complexion is pale. Five days have passed since Emily lost her battle with the White Death. And with this loss a piece of my Cora has died.

I tentatively move closer to her. She places her hand against my chest and holds my gaze before I feel both her arms wrap under my coat and around my waist and back. I hold her for how long, I do not know, as she rests her head against my shoulder.

CHAPTER EIGHT

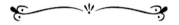

September 1854
Eli, Age 17

 e hold hands as we walk toward the lake. I stumble.

"What's wrong?" Cora asks.

"I do not know." I bend down toward my leg. It aches. "My leg. It feels . . ." Terrified, I look up at her as I grasp my shin. *No!* I think. "Hold my hand Cora!" She is frightened. I reach for her, our fingertips touch, but I am being pulled away from her. She runs toward me, but I am receding too quickly. I focus on her sorrowful eyes until she is gone.

May 1863
Eli, Age 26

I sit erect in this godforsaken cave, confused. My torturer is sitting on my left thigh with his back to me.

"Almost," I hear him say. I feebly pound his back with my bound fists. His shoulders jerk, a pop rattles through my leg, and my entire body spasms from the pain of my bones meshing together.

I surrender to the unrelenting burn of the whiskey as it washes through the wound. My mind spins. Gently he lifts his weight off my leg, and as I open my eyes again, I see a bearded colored man towering over me. He is smiling as if happy to see me.

He bends down next to me with the noxious cloth in hand.

"No," I beg.

"Had to set the bone again, you move around too much. You *do* want to walk again, do you not?"

"Please," I say. "Cora."

My face is covered again. I hold my breath for as long as I can, but it is no use.

"Go," he says grinning, "be with your Cora."

I loathe this man.

December 1854
Eli, Age 17

The morning fog wisps around us as we walk a familiar path to Cora's home.

"I worry for my mother," Cora says. "She has spoken not more than a dozen words to me in as many days." I squeeze her hand. "And since Father left for Massachusetts last September, she has no one to care for. I fear she has lost herself. She knits and knits and knits. I can hardly take it. Have you any idea how many sweaters I have?" I wrap an arm around her waist and pull her close.

"I suppose there are worse things."

"Indeed," she says.

At our backs we hear a faint gallop. As we approach Cora's home a mounted expressman trots up. He stiffly dismounts his horse.

His brim hat sits just above his eyebrows. A blue scarf covers his mouth and nose for shielding the crisp air from smarting his face and lungs. He pulls the scarf down, exposing a burly mustache.

"Good morning, may I inquire about the Hannah residents?" he asks.

"I am Miss Hannah."

"Well, Miss, I have a letter for a Samantha."

"That would be me."

He hands the letter to her while I rummage through a few coins in my pocket to pay him.

"Beg your pardon," he says. "Seems I am the better part of two months late. A number of parcels have been delayed from Massachusetts. Such dismal clime."

"It is a letter from Father," Cora whispers. "Sir, I am

happy to have it, tardy or not. May I impart an extra blanket or two for you and your horse? We have recently come into a surplus beyond our handling."

"Miss, no, thank you, I would not take advantage of your generosity."

"It is no trouble; if you would be so kind as to stay just one moment . . ." She slips inside before he is able to muster a fuss.

"Where are you from?" I ask.

"Virginia," he says proudly. "Well, I should say originally from Virginia, but I have been on the trails for so very long. Home is where I am sleeping for the night." He points at the Hannah residence. "I say, you have a keeper there in that one. If I may be so bold."

I nod.

"Could not help but notice her finger is missing the Lord's ring."

"I have yet to ask her hand," I say with some embarrassment.

He frowns. "Well, get to it, boy. Take it from an old coot that has made his mistakes. You are fortunate beyond compare and have yet to realize it."

Moments later, Cora returns with two large blankets, a mug of nearly scalding tea, and a half-dozen carrots hanging from their leaves.

I relieve her of the steaming mug as she hands the blankets to the expressman. He flanks his horse with the larger of the two, and then drapes the other around his shoulders.

"Much obliged, Miss Hannah." His face flushes bright pink. I hand him the drink.

"Oh, it burns," he gasps as the heat touches his near-frozen fingers.

"My apologies," Cora says.

"No, not at all. It is a good burn."

Cora pets the horse's neck under the freshly placed blanket. "May I?" she asks, as she dangles the carrots in front of the horse.

"She would love them."

"What is her name?" she asks.

"This is Victoria—goes by Vicki. She is a great listener. Keeper of all my secrets." He smiles. Cora continues to pet Vicki's neck as she chomps on the carrots. I have yet to meet a horse that did not appreciate Cora. She has always been able to bend the ear of most animals.

Cora whispers something in Vicki's ear, which neither the expressman nor I can hear. Vicki neighs.

Cora looks at me knowingly. "A little girl talk."

"Perhaps my secrets are in danger," the expressman says as he adjusts his newly acquired blanket. "Well, I best be on my way. Miss, I must say knowing that there are decent and kind folks like you and yours in this world, it warms my heart."

"But what of your wife?" she asks. A thin uncomfortable smile falls across his lips. "No . . . cannot claim that I have one. I used to in another life, well, nearly did. When I was a boy probably about your age, I . . . she went away—*I went away.*"

He turns toward me and reaches to shake my hand. The warmth of the mug has heated his palm considerably. "I will be on my way, Mister . . .?" he says softly.

"Eli West."

"Coleman Bellflowers," he says as he releases my hand. "Mister West, with this young lady at your side, you may be the richest man in America." He nods and turns away.

"Mister Bellflowers, I almost forgot!" Cora exclaims. "I have something else for you."

"Please, no, you have done so much—" But it is too late. She has vanished beyond the doorway. I turn to him with a smile, but I am met with a pointed finger. "Do remember what I have told you," he says. "I waited, and look where it has gotten me. I love the open road and my Vicki here," he says as he rubs her side. "But, if I could do it all over again, I would have married my girl, staked a claim out West, and given old Vicki here what she deserves—rolling hills of wild grass. Waiting will turn you into an old, lonely man. Do not postpone. The cherry blossoms are around the corner."

I nod.

Once again Cora returns, but this time she carries two warm loaves of bread.

"We cannot let you leave without something baked. It just would not be right." He nods graciously as he accepts them and is rather speechless for a few seconds.

"Thank you kindly, Miss Hannah," he gushes.

Cora and I embrace each other and look on as the expressman maneuvers Vicki back onto the trail. Soon the fog engulfs them, and we are alone.

"That was really sweet of you," I say as we approach the porch steps. "What moved you to such generosity?"

"He was in need. His fingers were cold and gnarled from holding the reins. What would you expect that I do? When we lose our kindnesses . . ." she pauses. "What did Mister Bellflowers impart upon your impressionable ears while I fetched his bread?"

"He told me that you are a keeper and that I should marry you under cherry blossoms."

"Is that so?" she says as her eyes meet mine. "What if I do not wish to *wait* for the cherry blossoms?"

CHAPTER NINE

September 1854
Eli, Age 17

Clouds weigh heavy above us, and although the rain has just been drizzles today, our path is sodden. I feel the wheels give along the pebbled path as our stagecoach sways. The town's priest sits quietly next to my father in the driver's box with a worn Bible on his lap. The horses neigh as my father commands them to a steady trot.

Cora's warmth presses against my side, and as I gaze across from me I witness a mother lost in thought. She has both hands on Emily's casket.

Missus Hannah's grief is hidden behind black lace. Cora dons no such adornment. She pulls her hair from her face, exposing raw eyes, and holds my hand tightly.

My eyes drift to the rear of the wagon. Fence posts, old and rotted, recede as we solemnly ride toward Emily's resting place. Yesterday morning I spent some hours digging the plot. As I gaze upon the dark dirt still under my fingernails, I think of a child's tiny smile, childish giggles.

The swaying soon stops as the horses come to a halt. I look into Cora's eyes and caress the release of my hand. At the rear of the carriage my father waits for me. Steadying myself against the wagon, I reach for Cora, guiding her step to the ground, while my father obliges to help Missus Hannah.

They enter the field as my father and I gently retrieve Emily's remains. We are the only pallbearers.

The plot is nearly one hundred yards from the road. This is to be a small ceremony. Just the priest and the four of us are to attend.

Father and I place the casket at Emily's grave. I move close to Cora and put my arm around her waist. As the priest commences with the ceremony, I think to myself that Cora's father should be here.

The priest raises his hand, pulling me from my righteous thoughts. Cora struggles to remain upright as she weeps into an ornately laced handkerchief. The orator nods toward my father, and then me, signaling that we lower Emily's body into the plot.

I pull away from Cora and meet my father. We feed two ropes beneath either end of the casket. I hold my ends and raise the casket a few inches from the ground. Father matches me, and we carefully lower Emily into the earth.

As we retrieve the ropes, a final prayer is read, and Cora falls to her knees. Her hands mash the wet earth. As she raises them, they seem to float above her sister as the soil sifts through her fingers. Soon, Missus Hannah is at our side casting clumps of soil and gilded prayers to a loving daughter that was.

CHAPTER TEN

May 1843
Eli, Age 6

Thereis a certain way to loop a worm on a hook so that it does not perish a few moments after it is pierced.

"Eli," my mother would say, seizing my wandering attention, "like this. You see? Otherwise, our worm will not wriggle in the water for very long. Fishes, in this lake especially, enjoy wriggly worms for breakfast."

Mostly what I remember about her is her touch and the softness of her skin. I am older now, and she is gone. I loop a worm through the hook not knowing if I have done it right. I wish she were here to observe my worm hooking. With dangling toes skimming the water I check the line and cast it into the lake.

Sometimes when I hold my breath I can hear her whispers. Sometimes when I doze on the deck I feel her combing my hair.

My naked feet patter against the soil as I hurry back to the house. The sun is too high. I am late. I hear the slap of the front door as my father waits for me on the porch. I had not buried the dinner bones from last night, nor had I swept the house of dirt.

I stand near the bottom step of the porch. He walks toward me. I step back, fearing a switching.

"Papa, I caught four fish!" I feign. He pulls the bucket from my fingers, along with the fishing pole, and sets them along a step.

Sighing deeply, his massive hands grab my shoulders. "Boy, what did I tell you about your chores?"

I sulk, "But, Papa, Mo—"

He shakes me. "Boy, do not start. She is not down at the lake. She does not wait for you in your dreams! Your mother is dead!" I believe he is not yet completely convinced of his own words. But it still hurts, so I cry. I know that she *is* here. I have felt her.

I shut my eyes to my father's rage, and within the darkness I see her perched behind him on the porch steps. She extends her hand toward him. She touches his shoulder. I feel the blissful warmth of her love.

His hold abruptly releases from me. After a moment, I wipe the tears from my cheeks and open my eyes to find not my father but a bucket of fish and my fishing pole. I gather them up and fetch after my chores.

CHAPTER ELEVEN

May 1863
Eli, Age 26

I wake to the scent of Mississippi gumbo. Haunting shadows dance along the cave walls by the light of the fire. The gumbo whets my appetite, but my thirst is stronger. I rub my face, cringing as the pain in my mouth pulses. I roll my tongue across the upper right-hand side of my mouth and find that all teeth are missing: molars to incisors. I panic as I roll my tongue again against jellied blood. Instinctively, a fingertip delicately rubs along the gum line. As I bring the finger to my eye, inspecting it for blood, I realize that my hands are unbound. I shake nervously for fear that I am being watched this whole time. I raise myself, but barely, as I am still absent my strength. I might have lost thirty pounds.

No one is watching me. For the first time that I know of, I am alone in this rocky cell. I try to roll on my side but my left leg is splinted clear up to my thigh. I lie flat again, and as my right hand falls to the side, I hear a ping. At my right is a warm bowl of gumbo, a spoon, and a tin of water. My arms nearly fail me as I try not to knock over the water. I sit up best I can and slurp at it. The wetness hurts my torn gums, but I endure it to an empty tin. I feel like I am going to vomit, but I continue; the food is too enticing. I spoon the gumbo to my mouth. I miss most of it. But at least I am able to consume the flavor. Maybe I hastily passed judgment on my captor. Maybe he is less of a monster than I think. After a few minutes and many missed spoonfuls I lie back down. It is only now that I taste not chloroform but an aftertaste of something else. Something. An indomitable sleepiness falls over me. Perhaps I have not misjudged anything.

December 1854
Eli, Age 17

September 19th, 1854

My Dearest Samantha,

The nights have become unbearable. I have been neglectful in this writing for the better part of a week. Tonight, however, I cannot allow another to pass without putting these words to paper.

I have addressed this letter to you for fear that your mother will leave it untouched or perhaps not accept it.

I must beg your forgiveness and that of your mother. Had I not brought my sickness into our home, your sister might still be in our lives. It is for this reason I must stay in Massachusetts indefinitely.

You are a grown woman—fully capable of caring for a home. I am not worried about your ability to cope. I know this may come as unwelcome tidings, but it seems the best way not to further curse my loved ones.

I will regularly send money in your care. It will not be be-fitting of what you and Mother deserve, but it will sustain the creature comforts that we have been accustomed to.

Please, my dearest, be gentle with your mother.

Love,

Papa

CHAPTER TWELVE

May 1863
Eli, Age 26

The morning light wakes me from Mister Hannah's letter. Today, if my eyes met him, I might call him a coward.

I feel a burning in my groin. I must handle my necessaries. I must pee now. Had my captor been obliging me these last few days? I hiss through my teeth—what is left of them, anyway, as I try to figure the best way to relieve myself. At my side, I find not poison gumbo but a pot for just such a necessity, and the tin filled with water again. I slide the pot over to me as best I can, tilt it, and . . . I wish I could say I do not miss.

I am still alone. The pot and water did not set themselves. I grab the water tin. Smell it for a moment before I gulp it down. Although the last gumbo was peppered with some concoction, it did ease my ravenousness appetite. I am still hungry and thirsty, but I feel less like an animal now, and have the luxury of inspecting my drink and food—to some measure—before it meets my tongue. After maybe an hour I am still awake, and I see no sign of him.

My mind drifts. I think of Cora. I am tired again. And for the first time in days I surrender to the overwhelming approach of sleep, without poison on my breath.

February 1847
Eli, Age 10

My father opens the door to a ten-year-old girl in a light blue dress. Cora's soiled toes peek out from the hem as she sways her hips softly. My father can be an intimidating presence to nearly any man, to say nothing of a child. She steps back and tilts her head nearly straight up to meet his eyes.

"Samantha," my father says, "how come you insist on not wearing shoes?"

"Mister West," she says courageously, "I believe them to be greatly overrated." A breeze blows over the porch as her reddish hair floats across half her face, leaving one piercing blue eye steely and bright staring into him.

"Well, okay, my dear. Your boyfriend awaits." My father gestures her to come in.

"Papa! She is *not* my girlfriend!" I say bitterly as I appear from his side.

Cora smiles. Her freckles seem to sparkle as she recognizes me, but before a smudged toe crosses the threshold, a palm pressing upon her shoulder stops her cold.

"Wait a minute," booms my father's voice. Cora's smile drains as a splinter of fright washes over her. It seems for a moment she might be eaten by the man above her. "What did we talk about the other day?" He gestures toward a pail full of water just a few feet away.

Cora pouts as she shamefully walks to the pail, gathers her dress up to her knees, and plunks one foot, and then the other, into the water.

"Scrub them well, child," my father says. While obliging him, a flush of embarrassment floods her cheeks. She reaches for a towel hanging from the railing, and then begins to dry her feet. "I cannot have dirt spread around my home."

"I know," she mumbles.

"Samantha, have I not told you a dozen times? Just wear your shoes, and then when you come for a visit, take them off and set them here." He points to the shoe corner to the left.

Now out of the pail and with dry feet she stands before him again. Her arms rise above her head. Her legs lift her to the balls of her feet as she spins elegantly, and then bows to the keeper of the gate.

"Kind sir, may I now enter?"

My father places his hand upon her shoulder and pulls her into me. "Go play, Eli," he says. "You better watch out for this one. She has all the trappings of a troublemaker."

DREAMS OF ELI

A crisp breeze rushes past me as I prop open my bedroom window. Cora snoops around my room. Her eyes dance across my collection of books while her fingertips rap against the worn spines. She stops with her back to me as she muses over the dresser top.

Before I am able to stop her, her fingers trace a daguerreotype of my mother. It is one of the few keepsakes left of my mother. Cora seems intrigued as she studies the woman looking back at her. Although the image is weathered, few would doubt her beauty. Cora spins around hugging the frame to her chest. I am guarded as I reach for it.

"Do not worry," she says. "I will not drop her." But I am worried. "You never mentioned her name."

I hesitate. "Amelia."

"Tell me more about her. You only told me that she died because she was sick. What was she like?"

"I am not really sure. Papa . . . does not speak of her much. That was taken six months before she died. I was three."

"Your father—"

"I stopped asking years ago. My questions only upset him. All I know is she got sick. Influenza or some such."

"Do you remember anything more?"

"I am pretty sure that I remember her smell and taking walks in the rain."

Thinking about her makes me weak, like my bones are being hollowed. Cora places the frame on the dresser.

She spins around slowly on one foot, and putting her finger to her chin, she nibbles her bottom lip. Curious, I sit up with my hands firmly on the bed.

"I have a question," she says as the sun's golden light kisses her face. "Do you know about Saint Valentine's Day?"

"No, not much."

"But Mister West . . . oh."

"If he did, I do not remember anything about it."

"Well, it is one of the most magical days, besides Christmas." She walks toward me until our knees touch. "Eli, will you be my valentine?" She seems vulnerable.

"When is it?"

"Next Sunday, the fourteenth, so you have a whole week to prepare." She leans in closer, eager for me to accept.

"But what do I have to do?"

"You could write me a poem, maybe buy me my favorite confections; flowers would be lovely."

"That sure seems like a lot of work. What do I get in return?"

"Well . . . me," she says meekly. Her purity seems to emanate from deep pools of innocence. I want to hug her, but I am afraid if I do I may melt into her, utterly losing myself.

"I think you have found your valentine," I whisper in her ear. She squeals with excitement that cannot be contained and wrestles me to the bed, covering every inch of my face with little kisses. "Wait," I say, "what is your favorite confection?"

"Lots of chocolate."

CHAPTER THIRTEEN

May 1863
Eli, Age 26

I feel a tremor as my body fights to wake. I gaze to my right. The tin has not been refilled, nor has the pot been emptied.

I am hungry again, but I do not see or smell anything. It seems it has been only a couple hours since I last dozed. I still have ten-year-old Cora and me swimming within the waves of my mind.

I reach for my wedding ring. Out here it is the only remnant I have left of her. In my soldiering I always carried her daguerreotype with me. Every evening I would pull her gaze from my breast pocket and whisper the day's doings to her. But on one particularly brutal and unforgiving day, I reached for her and found only folds of fabric. She had fallen away. I felt as though I had lost myself all over again.

Although our home resides upon my father's land, and

Cora's earthly belongings are well kept, that life is easily one hundred miles south of here. In my present condition I must recognize that that life may be beyond my reach. This ring—as long it is here with me, I still have a piece of her.

Thirst burns my throat as I focus on the embers of the spent fire. To my delight a whiskey bottle teases me from ten feet away. I backstroke as if in my childhood lake and inch myself toward the bottle. I feel the bones in my shattered leg mill against each other. I search for a stick to wedge between my teeth, and then laugh—I am missing the requisite molars to make such a device useful. In lieu of the needed teeth, and a stick for that matter, I continue across the unforgiving ground on my rib-riddled back. About five minutes later, my left hand wraps around the Old Orchard. I pop the cork and gulp two-and-a-half fingers' worth. My breath turns to fire as I wheeze and hack. I rest the left side of my face against a rock warmed by the lulled fire and discover I have underestimated the strength I have lost from my ten-foot journey. My body is limp as the alcohol works through me. I close my eyes and recede into slumber.

February 1855
Eli, Age 18

My father walks his future daughter-in-law over flower petals. As I stand with our priest clothed in his finest godly robe, I think of Mister Bellflowers—the expressman from Virginia. I wish I could tell him that I am not in the wait, that I will not be alone in this life.

The grass is damp from the winter's day. Cora had

insisted that the wedding be outside. I look to the sky and admire plumes of cotton clouds blotting the deepest blue. As I absorb this beauty, I feel God with me.

My father holds the hand of my love as they approach me. He nods in my direction, and then turns to Cora, lifting her veil and kissing her twice. Once on each blushing cheek.

"Sebastian," she whispers, "thank you for being my papa too."

"Honored to," he says, and then takes his rightful place next to me as my best man.

A wry smile crosses Cora's face as I reach for her hand. She peers down at her dress. It engulfs her, but unknown to our wedding party, save Father and me, bare feet stained of grass and earth peek out from underneath the waves of wedding dress.

I wish I could say I remember everything about the ceremony, but I do not. It is mostly a jumble in my mind. As I slip the ring over her finger she begins to cry. I wipe her cheek, and I try to kiss her.

"No," says my father.

I see her lips move, repeating holy promises. My hand is steady as I feel her touch and watch the gold ring slowly slide to the base of my finger. I feel myself falling into her eyes.

I hold her waist with my hands, her warmth with my heart, and her lips with a kiss. There is a hush, and then amusement blushes throughout our gathering as my wife exposes a dirty bare foot for all to see.

CHAPTER FOURTEEN

May 1863
Eli, Age 26

As he enters, I can feel him looking at me. I stifle the urge to squirm about, hoping that if I refrain from moving he will leave me be. It seems I cannot help but slowly crack my eyelids.

"Oh, good, you are awake," he says as he takes a step toward me. I flinch with great agony as the pain from my leg ripples through me. "Do not move that leg. I would not want to have to set it again. I do not believe you want that either." He takes another step forward. "Hope you like bass." He dangles two large fish over my head. I am wide-eyed and still a little drunk. He bends down closer to me. I flinch again, gripping my blankets, and recognize that I am no longer by the fire pit with a bottle in hand. He must have carried me back to my makeshift cot. I study him with a frantic eye. He holds a hand up as if to show he is not a threat. The man is shirtless—and a Negro as dark as I ever saw.

"No," I say desperately as I try to back away, but I surrender to the pain.

With a stern eye, he says, "We have gone through this a dozen times. You still do not recognize me?"

I look into his eyes. It cannot be.

"Ezra?"

"Close your eyes," he says. I am untrusting and do not dare. "Listen to my voice," he says as he walks back to the table and sets down the fish. "Do you remember the day we became friends? It was my birthday, and you asked me what my parents gifted me. Then I told you nothing because 'property does not get presents.' Do you remember that?"

I nod. "I took you to the lake for the first time that day."

"Yes, you did," he says.

"But I could have told you about my childhood while in the throes of torture and under the *darkness*," I respond.

A hardy laugh escapes him. I do not know this voice; I do not remember this laugh.

"Torturing you?" he says. "You mean *helping* you. Yes, you did tell me a lot of things. But my birthday never came up. You had more pressing things to tell." He pauses for a moment. "Sorry I was not here for you when you found yourself alone."

My eyes burn in his direction. I do not want him to say her name again.

"Examine your leg for yourself. It is healing. I removed the ball and have washed the wound. You lost some bone, but it should grow back. You are lucky, considering the damage."

"But what about my mouth, my bound wrists?" I say as I remember the tearing of my gums and the unmerciful pulling of my teeth. The mere thought makes my broken gums pulse.

"You smashed your face against a boulder when you collapsed. A good amount of your teeth were shattered. To leave them to further cut your mouth would have been unkind. You still have a festering case of mouth rot. The Old Orchard will help to lessen the overall ache. However, it will not last much longer since you found nearly the bottom of it."

Things seem to be making more sense, but I still have questions. If this is Ezra, it is the first time I have seen him in nearly nine years. Where has he been? But before I figure him out, I still have to figure me out. "Did you shoot me?" I ask.

"Sorry, yes," he confesses. "At four hundred yards, all you Graybacks look the same."

I shudder as he walks toward me again, and with good reason, for every time he comes near, pain follows.

"No," I say as I raise my hand, but I am still too weak to fend off any approach.

"It is all right. I will not do anything you do not wish." He lays his hand upon my broken shin. I tense, anticipating the worst, but to my surprise, it is a gentle touch. After a moment he covers my leg. He rolls the blanket off my other foot. I am shocked to see bandages messily wrapped around the big toe.

Slowly he pulls the ribbons. With each loop unraveled a faint pink stains deeper and deeper, until the cloth turns to a wet-crimson. He sets them aside and begins his examination. I was unaware that my toe was missing all of its nail and a significant amount of flesh. Exposure to the air smarts the wound.

"Eli, you had a fester of gangrene that probably would have killed you in a few weeks. Good thing I shot you, huh?" I sigh, measuring my current situation and ponder the thought of death. Oddly, presently, I do not abhor it.

I think about how I came to be here. And as I study him, this apparent old friend of mine, my thoughts pull me into a place of deepening darkness. I think about how we are no longer carefree children, but rather men, recklessly sculpted by our failures, by our fears, and by the deeds we commit during the tumult of war.

"How long have I been here?"

"Five days, I reckon."

"Did you punch me in the face?" I say, pressing a puffy left eye.

He laughs again. "Yes, you would not shut your yap."

"I see."

"Do you like bass?" he asks again.

"Yes," I say perhaps too quickly.

"I know we have a lot to talk about, but first we must eat." He walks over to the table and begins to gut the fish. "Is there anything I can get you?"

"Water," I say.

A moment later he hands me the tin half full. "Anything else?"

"Yeah, but you are not going to like it." I cradle my concaved belly.

"Your necessaries? Ahh, shit."

"Exactly."

April 1855
Eli, Age 18

As a younger man I had worked in Mister Codwell's general store as a stock boy. But with my new marital status, he seems to see me in a new light and has offered me a position as his bookkeeper. Had I not been besotted with my future wife and her mathematical skill all those years ago, it is doubtful I would have been considered for such a trusted position.

Missus Hannah has always thought me worthy of her daughter's love. It seems with my new position, and with her daughter's love fully committed to me, she has been engaging me in particularly lively conversations. Perhaps I am filling some gap left by her absent husband.

I am trying *not* to learn knitting. Since moving in with

Cora and her mother, I have darned seven pairs of my own socks. On top of the socks and scribing numbers, I assist the building of our new home. My father had insisted it be built upon his land, to which I willingly obliged. But I do fear that the darning will continue even beyond the completion of our new home.

Perhaps Missus Hannah's resolve that I learn the art of knitting is her way of ensuring I will never be without proper socks or the like, if, God forbid, I ever find myself alone in this world.

Lately, Cora expresses her concerns over her mother's circumstances, but I fail to see a problem. It is clear that she will join us in our new home upon its completion.

As for Cora's father, we have yet to receive any other correspondence since the one parcel last December. To my knowledge, he has yet to make arrangements for his forgotten family. I have been making the monthly allotments for what is needed in our daily lives; a charge I willingly embrace.

I wake to my wife violently retching in the water closet. The moon casts its light upon my face as I wait to hear her again, dispelling the thought that I am still dreaming. And again I hear her. I roll from the bed and stagger toward her direction. The morning light will not rise for a few hours yet.

I tap the door as I push it forward. Cora is on her side holding a washcloth to her mouth and leaning over a wash pot. Another round hits her. I pour her a glass of water, and after the kecking settles, I help her sit up.

"Thanks," she says as she sips. "I am feeling better now." Her damp skin is luminous under the moonlight. I pull aside wet strands of hair from her cheeks.

"What happened?"

"I was sleeping, but woke with a start. Had I not rushed to the wash here, I would have made a terrible mess of our bed."

"Was it supper that upset you?"

"No," she says, "I do not believe I am sick. I mean, I do—I am sick. Obviously one would not spit up unless . . ." I feel her forehead. It is warm but not feverish.

"I will send for the doctor at first light." I feel her head again. She pulls my hand down and lightly kisses it. A moment of joy washes over her face. "What is it?" I ask.

"It is not consumption."

"I have said no such thing."

"Yes, Love, but you thought it. I am perfectly normal. I have been waiting . . ."

"Tell me."

"Help me up. I think I am finished with this unforgiving floor." She presses her body against me as we stand. I place my hands on her hips as she rests her head against my neck. "Eli," she says, "when is our home going to be ready?"

"Certainly not any longer than July."

"Good," she says softly necking me with kisses.

"Why? I thought you liked it here?"

I hold her closer as she pulls one of my hands from her hips and rests it just under her navel. "I had my suspicions, but I wanted to wait before I told you. I wanted to be sure," she whispers. "I have not bled since a week before our wedding." My knees buckle as I absorb her words. "Yes," she says.

"I am a father?"

"Soon, and me a mommy," she beams, trying to contain her excitement. I am not so disciplined, and I shout to any and all that can hear.

"Shhh, you will wake Mother."

"I want to wake the entire town!" As we hold each other we weep until we find ourselves giggling like the carefree children we used to be.

CHAPTER FIFTEEN

May 1863
Eli, Age 26

L ooking back on it," Ezra says as he spoons stew into his mouth, "I do regret what I did. I should have just run away and been done with it."

"But he would have found another boy and another," I say as I slurp my spoonful. It has been a week since my discovery of my old friend.

"Perhaps," he says pensively as he considers my words. "I wish I could say the doctor was my one and only miscalculation, but there have been a few others. More than a few, if you include the war." He looks at me. "I assure you I have never harmed another man without it being just. Yet, my soul is not at ease." I say nothing, as I too reflect. "Eli, do you believe in Heaven?" Had he asked me this question eight years ago, with a pregnant angel for a wife and the world before me, I would have said *of course*, without hesitation. But instead, I answer him with a question.

"Why?"

"I want to think that despite all the wrongs I have committed that I still have a chance."

"Ezra, if you are denied and find yourself outside the gates of Heaven, I have a feeling I will be at your side."

"This does not comfort me," he says.

"The book says 'Thou Shall Not Murder,' but what about war? When I am faced with the enemy, I have to choose, him or me. And in that moment, I do not wish my own demise. I confess, I have thought about death and leaving all of this life behind me, but in the moment when I am shoulder to shoulder with a man that wants me dead, I would rather him go first. I do not want to kill him, but what choice am I left with?"

"What about the other choice?" he asks.

"What is that?"

"Both simply lay down their weapons."

"Yes, but when have you seen or done such a thing?"

Ezra stares at me with cold acceptance. "I am doing it right now, *Grayback*."

"Yes—but, *we* are brothers."

"We are all brothers."

June 1847
Eli, Age 10

"I can make a stone skip like a frog hops lilies," I brag as I flick a dancing piece of granite across the water. Cora's eyes sparkle as it carves expanding concentric circles along the surface.

Her feet dig into the bank. Wet sand squishes between her toes as she launches a flat rock. The lake swallows it without a hint of mercy. An impatient frown steels her face.

"Flick it," I say for what could be the hundredth time.

"I did. It gulped it again, you saw it," she says. She combs the sand for yet another projectile. A cool breeze seems to smooth her frustrations away. "Eli, why do you come here?" she asks sincerely.

I look down at the bank. "Ezra and I . . . habit, I suppose."

"No, I do not believe this is the reason. I watch you when you think I am in my own thoughts."

"You watch me?" I say.

"There is nothing queer about me paying attention. You seem to drift, and sometimes I notice a flicker in your eyes as you gaze into the woods, like you are waiting for something." I continue to scout for the perfect stone, not wanting to face her.

"If I tell you, you may consider me an odd stick."

"Too late," she says with a giggle. "For some time now I have known you are three coppers short of a dime." I look toward the woods, cloaking my sorrow with a smile that mars my soul.

"My mother used to come here." I scoop up a random rock and toss it along the surface water. This time it plunks into the deep. "It is not like I talk to her." I hesitate. "I used to think she was here." I feel as though I am in the buff telling her this. I wait for her sharp tongue. But that is not Cora. She is not cruel. Despite her kindness, however, I feel I have given away a piece of me and regret settles into my bones.

"When you see her again, will you tell me?" This strange regret continues to weigh upon me, weakening me further as if being eaten from the inside out.

"Yes," I say, "but now that I am older, I do not believe she is here. I no longer have the fantasy of a six-year-old." This is perhaps the only lie I have ever told Cora. Perhaps I am trying to protect my memories.

Cora is pensive as she embraces me. I should feel loved, but I cannot remember a time when I felt more alone.

"I *believe*," she says, as she rests her head against my shoulder.

CHAPTER SIXTEEN

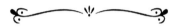

May 1863
Eli, Age 26

I wake with irritation.

"Ezra?"

"Yeah?"

"How close is the waterfront from here?"

"You are not strong enough, and I would rather you not put any weight on your leg yet."

"I did not ask you if you thought I should put weight on my leg. I asked how far the waterfront is."

"Someone is grumpy. Trust me, it is not time. You do not want to separate that bone again."

"I need you to take me to the lake."

"Why would I do that?"

"Because I have been steeped here in my own filth for

twenty days by my shaky count. Have you ever lay in one spot for twenty days? I smell so bad I do not even want to be around myself. How can you stand to be around me?" He seems to contemplate my question, perhaps sensing the desperate tenor in my voice.

"It is true your cleanliness is lacking but—"

"But nothing," I say. "You ripped out a significant amount of my teeth, carved my big toe like a piece of meat, and you shot me. *You* shot me. You must take me to the water's edge. I cannot be here another day without at least a break. This unforgiving gritstone is killing me."

"You have the lot of blankets."

"They are failing," I tell him bluntly. He rolls a couple blankets off my leg and presses in all the wrong places. I squint and suck, filling my lungs, hoping that the pain will abate shortly.

"You see, Eli, I merely touched you."

"I do not care. I am *rotting* here." Ezra unravels some of the bandages around my leg. Judging by his furrowing brow he does not like what he sees.

"You do have a festering." He dresses it again and moves over to my other foot. "Your toe is scabbing nicely." The toe repulses me oddly even more so than my bloody leg. He tilts my head back and examines his dentistry. I huff. "Ahh, your breath is foul."

"Blood, gumbo, and days-old bark juice. Take me to the lake," I say.

He rubs his beard as he forms his diagnosis. "Okay,

yes." I had expected to argue more and am stunned by this sudden reversal. "You ready?" he asks.

"Wait. Why the sudden change?" He looks at me with an air of concern.

"Recently I have poured water over a few wounds with days-old pus. Sometimes it helps. I am hoping that a good wash in the lake will reduce the rotting. Maggots seemed to work some too, but several men have told me the crawling at all hours can be unpleasant."

"Maggots?" I say.

"Yes, they eat the dead right out of you. Either way, something needs to be done. I suppose I could fill the pots and tins with water and rinse your wound here, but I would prefer to submerge your entire leg for a while."

"Agreed."

"You do realize that it is only May. The water is likely very cold." This is no concern to me. One way or another I am going to rid myself of my present condition.

"How are we doing this?" I ask.

"When I lift you, I need you to put all your weight on the heel of your right foot. Do *not* press any of your toes."

I nod. He stands over me as I reach for him. He pulls me up like I am a child. I concentrate my weight upon my right heel. A dizzy spell spins me for a moment as he lowers his shoulder to my belly and gently pulls my heel from the ground. My leg burns, but I try not to complain. He wedges me over his shoulder, and as I dangle from him, my hip bones seem to carve into his muscular upper body.

"You smell like shit."

"*Thank you*," I say kindly.

I feel weightless as I float naked in cold water. If it were not for my broken leg, my swollen jaw, and half big toe, I might be fooled into believing Heaven has found me. Clouds float above me as the sun hugs my face. I feel a peace I have not felt since I was a young man.

Ezra ruins my bliss, holding my leg and softly rubbing the sickly flesh. The coldness deadens some of the pain, but it is not near cold enough to allow me to continue to embrace my newfound peace.

"Almost done," he assures me.

A moment later I am floating away from him and am alone with my thoughts. I feel a breeze upon my exposed skin. It chills me, but I welcome it. I see trees silently sway all around as my ears submerge under the water. As my flesh seems to soak in the beauty surrounding me, a silence builds within my mind. I close my eyes and before long, she comes to me, Cora. She sweetly sings to me, but nothing from her lips meets my ears. I hear only the hushing water of the lake. The mere sight of her lips, her dark locks, her brilliance, educes a familiar, raw sorrow within me.

After a while I feel a tug on my hand. Ezra tows me back to the shallows. Over his shoulder is linen.

"Here, wrap this around you," he says, as he helps

secure it around my floating body. He hoists me back over his shoulder. As he situates me, I feel nearly weightless, like a paper doll. The water settles, and as I stare at it, I find myself looking into the sunken beady orbs that were once a man's eyes. His jaw is swollen, and his skin is taut and sickly. As I reach for him, he reaches for me too. We both examine our arms and are equally horrified by what we see. They are weak and emaciated. By my count, he is likely three days from the bone orchard.

As Ezra pulls me away from him, my fingertips skim the water. And I cannot help but feel empathy for the man dying in the lake.

September 1855
Eli, Age 18

I plunge my hands into a pail on the patio. Water spills over its lip when I wring the handkerchief. As I lay the handkerchief along the porch banister, I shake my hands dry and pray that the blood will stop.

"Can I make you more comfortable?" I quietly ask. Cora holds her belly with both hands and tries to sing a lullaby. I have never felt so helpless. I pull her hair from her face. Her breathing is raspy.

I remove my shoes and socks, untie my trousers, lift

the blankets, and slide in behind her, spooning her body with mine. My hand trails her arm, and then rests on her belly. I kiss her neck and begin to sing her lullaby to our child. I feel her wheeze. She coughs into a handkerchief. The muffled breaths smell of medicine and sickness. Her body heaves. I continue to sing as I rub her hands and belly. I listen to her whispers as she tries to sing along. I try to conceal the tears in my eyes from her.

"Promise me," she says. "Promise me you will sing to her every night."

I caress her cheek and pull her toward me as I look deep into her eyes. So much pain swims within them. But I see her. And she sees me. I kiss her because I would rather die a sickly death with her than live in a world without her warmth and without her love.

CHAPTER SEVENTEEN

June 1863
Eli, Age 26

I wake to a troubled face. Ezra sits with his elbows pressed into his thighs and a hand to his chin. I feel him measuring me as his mesmerizing stare burrows into my leg.

"What is it?" I ask. His nose flares like I said something to upset him. "What?" I ask again.

"You smell that?"

"No," I say.

"You have a stench about you."

"Since when did your nose ginger? I cannot be that unbearable. It has only been a week since the lake," I quip, hoping that he will suggest another scrub.

"I should have done it at the start," he grumbles.

"Should have what?" I ask. He stands, and then walks over to me.

"Eli, I have some really bad news. But there is some light too."

"Give me the light."

"I am seventy percent confident that you are going to live."

"I said give me the light."

"That is it." He takes a knee and places a hand on my leg. The pressure pains me. "Eli . . . I am going to cut your leg off."

"HELL YOU ARE!"

"This is the only way I can save you," he says, as if trying to convince himself.

"But you have not examined me since yesterday morning. How can you be so rash when you have not even seen it?" I clamor for the right words.

"Eli, I can smell it. I know this smell. I know it too well." He tears my bandages, exposing my scarlet wet flesh. Immediately, a crippling stench strikes me, and I cannot help but turn away. "You see this?"

I look back and barely recognize my own leg. Some of the flesh has turned, displaying shades of chartreuse and deep violet. He peels back a small flap of skin, exposing a blackening area. I inhale a hiss, anticipating a mountain of pain. I feel nothing, only pressure.

"This will be your undoing," he says as he stares at me.

"I will do what is called the Circular Flap Method. It is the most advanced method known." I am unable to utter a word. "I will take it from here," he continues, as he touches just under my knee and traces his finger around the circumference of my upper calf. "It needs to be high enough above the wound to make sure I leave none of the sick area behind, but low enough to where I can fold a fair amount of skin and muscle over the bone."

"No," I whimper. "Please, Ezra." But I know he is right. I try to back away, but he holds my upper leg.

"I know that you are scared. But be assured you are safe in my hands. I am skilled in this kind of amputation. I have successfully managed hundreds of them, many not in such calm surroundings."

I breathe heavily as my mind begins to swoon. Surely I must be four shades of field grass by now. He is watchful as he stares into my terrified eyes. He then examines my leg further.

"What if . . ." I choke upon my chosen words. "What if you just let me go? Just let me go." My voice trails off as I begin to sob. Stinging tears pass over my cracked lips. But as I wallow in the acceptance of my own demise, I feel a wave of melancholy so beautiful that I am nearly swept into silence. Perhaps my enduring heartache will heal with my last earthly breath. *Perhaps* I will see her soon. He releases his hand from my thigh. He stands, but says nothing.

Abruptly, he leaves my side for the morning sunshine. I sigh into my bedding, relieved that he is gone.

After a few minutes Ezra returns and steadfastly

plunges an iron into the coals. He mumbles something caustic under his breath as he grabs for his satchel and turns his back to me. I cannot see what he is doing but grow increasingly apprehensive as I hear metal clashing together. He pulls a handkerchief from his back pocket.

"No," he says. "You are not thinking right. Your mind is clouded. You are speaking through agony."

He turns to me with that wicked bottle of chloroform and several saw blades spread out.

"NO!"

He pounces on me as I ineffectually try to wriggle away. My last memory as he smothers my face with the wet cloth is of splitting fingernails as I plunge them into the hardpan. The sting of my fingertips soon deadens, and so do I.

October 1855
Eli, Age 18

The soles of my shoes sink into the muddy earth as I collect wildflowers. Lord knows what blossoms comprise my growing bouquet. All I know is that they are colorful, and their scent speaks for me and my sentiments.

This time, instead of stomping my muddy boots against Cora's porch and handing my love her flowers, I rest them upon her stone and lower to my knees, feeling the soil with my hands.

Upon my shivering back, the warmth of a hand touches

me with a gentleness I have not felt in months—not since before Cora fell ill. I look up and see Missus Hannah. She sits and cradles my muddied hands in her lap. I squeeze her hand, her eyes so much like Cora's. For a moment the rain is our conversation.

"I did not keep secret my love for your daughter."

"Eli." She caresses my cheek with the back of her hand.

Before this grave in the rain, while holding the hand of a fallen mother, I am lost. I do not understand this world. I am not at peace.

CHAPTER EIGHTEEN

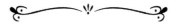

June 1863
Eli, Age 26

A s I wake a simmering fire casts a soothing light upon our surroundings. A thousand stars meet my eyes as I peer out the mouth of the cave.

I feel as if the devil's fingers press upon me as I lie nauseated. This sickness is all too familiar. An intense burning radiates from my broken leg. I try to rub my feet together, hoping for relief, but my right foot presses fabric.

I recall the smothering cloth in my face, the splitting fingernails. I roll the covers off my injured leg and slowly raise it against the firelight. I am no longer *all* of me. Bloody cloth ribbons dress only a stump. I am still swirling within myself from the chloroform, hoping and praying this is a dream. I know it is not. The pain I feel is different, though I no longer feel like I am dying. For the first time I am able to roll over to my right without difficulty.

As I lie on my side I think of what my life has become, what my future will bring. What is a man without a working leg? "Nothing," I sulk.

Ezra places his hand on my shoulder. My back is to him. He talks quietly. "Are you okay? Is it too much pain? Do you need more medicine?" I do not turn to him.

"I think you have done enough," I whisper back. He sighs as he releases his hand from my shoulder. I hear him retreat to his blankets. I have hurt him. It feels good to exact some pain in his direction, but almost immediately remorse lays its heavy hand. I begin to drift and hope that I have not cut too deeply the heart of the only true friend I have left.

November 1854
Eli, Age 17

She leans into me as we travel down a familiar path.

"Walk me to the water?" she asks. Her eyes are pained, red and raw.

"Sure," I say as we step toward an adjacent dirt trail. As we approach the water's edge she stops and casts her pale face to the sunlight. I step away from her. It seems she wants to be alone, but instinct tells me to stay. She bends to her knees, splashes her hands into the once calm cold water, and begins to sob.

I crouch next to her. A haunting cry chokes from her lungs. She falls into me, pushing me to the ground, her body trembling against mine. But soon she calms, and we hear only the hush of a breeze under the shining sun.

"Please tell me that she is here with us."

I close my eyes as she looks at me. I see Emily, wearing a yellow dress, barefoot and lovely. A single sunflower in her tiny hand bursts with sunlight. I reach for it, but my arms are pinned by her big sister's loving hug.

"She is here," I tell Cora as I open my eyes.

"I feel her too," she says as she returns her head to my chest. "I want to plant sunflowers in the spring." I caress her hair as we both close our eyes, and slowly she falls asleep in my arms.

CHAPTER NINETEEN

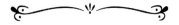

June 1863
Eli, Age 26

T he morning light intolerably pierces my eyes. Without my chloroform veil I feel the full pain surging from the stump of my missing appendage.

I turn toward Ezra's area but find only disheveled blankets. As I sit up, I discover the tin full with water again and an empty piss pot. I do feel different.

Was Ezra right? Perhaps this is best for me. I roll slowly onto my back, lifting my leg above me. What is left of it. I bring it to my fingertips and explore the plume of stained bandages. I pull at the end of a piece of material and watch as it starts to unravel.

With some work, I soon have a pile of bloodied cloth strips. I expect the worst—hacked and mangled flesh messily stitched, bone exposed. Growing up, I have never really

witnessed his medical prowess; certainly nothing as compli-
cated as an amputation.

I sigh at the loss of me. I am a mess. But still, even with
my untrained eye, I recognize the care he seems to have
taken. Many of my brothers suffered a similar fate. I believe
I would be envied by some.

Before, in my panicked state, when Ezra was explain-
ing the procedure, I was not able to absorb the words. As I
examine his work, I now understand why he prefers this
method. It appears the flesh and muscle that used to be my
calf has been pulled forward and sown to the front of the
shin. Hundreds of fine stitches have been meticulously
threaded into the skin. I press two fingers into the center of
the stump and wince as I discover swollen flesh—but not
bone. Perhaps I will feel it once the swelling simmers.

"No, not yet," Ezra admonishes as he enters the cave
with five fish and a long stick. He sets his bounty aside and
sits beside me, gathering the bandages. I look away, not
ready to face him. Silently, he begins to wrap my leg again.
His breathing is heavy as he manages the task. "Are they too
tight?"

I stare at the stone wall, avoiding him as best I can. I
am not ready to admit that I do feel better. The covers fall
upon me again, and within moments, the morning chill is
replaced by my body heat.

Sand crushes under his boots as he pivots back to the
makeshift table where the fish await. I listen as a blade
gnashes against the wood, severing their heads and gutting
their bellies with ease.

DREAMS OF ELI

Abruptly the carving stops. I then hear gritty footsteps coming toward me again. But this time I am not allowed to avoid him. As he bends down, he holds my shoulder flat against the blankets. Inside myself I am like a child throwing a tantrum.

"Eli," he says as he sets the stick across my chest, "I found this by the lake and thought you might have some use for it one day. I think the carving will be to your liking." His hand releases from my shoulder. In his eyes I see genuine concern. It is in this moment that I realize I have been fighting a friend.

I take hold of the stick and find on closer inspection that it is a walking staff with a knotted top. I believe the knot is supposed to wedge under my armpit. As I further survey its design, I marvel at the multitude of elaborate carvings.

"*You* carved this?" I ask. He pats my shoulder and nods. As he returns to the fish I feel some of the anguish inside me begin to lift like smoke. And in its place I am infused with gratitude. Is this forgiveness? I have often wondered what it would feel like. *True* forgiveness. Until now, such virtue seemed to have escaped me. I set the staff aside. "Thank you," I say weakly.

"Once you are able to move about by yourself I will leave here for a couple days and visit the Gallaway farm, just a day's walk from here. They are good people, kind to my skin. If I work double I am sure that you would be welcome too. Once you are bedded on the farm, I think you might be surprised how quickly you may recover. And once you feel righter and able to endure long travel, we will secure a couple horses and make for our journey home to Jackson. I am sure you would like to visit Samantha, and Mister West must wonder about you."

I nod, absorbing his words. "Yes," I say. "Yes, I would like that very much." He leaves me with my thoughts. And as I roll to my side warm within my blankets, I hear the sizzle of fish against an iron pan. Here, quietly, I think of what it would be like to be home again.

CHAPTER TWENTY

June 1863
Eli, Age 26

Although it has been only a few weeks since Ezra has removed my foot, he has decided to leave for the Gallaway farm.

I am recovering, but not quickly enough for his liking. He is certain I will do better under the ministrations of Catherine Gallaway.

It has been three days since his departure, and if he does not return by the morrow, I will fear he may have run into trouble and that I am on my own.

I hoped by now I would be walking around with ease, or I should say, hobbling around, but this is not to be. I am able to crawl and occasionally stand with my staff wedge firmly under the pit of my left arm. With this newfound freedom, it is rather refreshing to behold a different view than just cold stone.

I have yet to gain any weight, but I have hope. This day I am able to perch myself on a flat boulder just outside the cave. My fingertips rummage through a scrap serving of burnt fish.

I focus on the ground before me. My foot taps the soil while my missing appendage tries to follow its lead. A strange sensation then stretches my face. I am smiling. I cannot help but trace this welcome expression with my fingertips.

My chest huffs a loud, cavernous laugh as I cradle my boney ribcage with my hand. I think I may be losing my mind. I laugh even louder, thrusting my body into further fits of joyful aches and pains. My God, I am pathetic, withered, and worn.

As I dwell upon this, I hear the trot of horses. Within moments, Ezra rides up on a horse along with another in tow.

"What is this?" he says, referring to my changed disposition.

"Nothing," I chuckle.

"What is so funny?"

"Me, Ezra! Me! I am a mess!" He laughs, as he ties the horses to a nearby limb.

"Yes, you have been a mess in more ways than one."

He seats himself next to me and jovially bumps his shoulder against mine. "I would like to leave at first light."

"Reckon I will not be up for it, but yes, first light. I can smell the home cooking from here," I say.

"Good. Today I will concentrate on fattening you up." He turns and looks at my frailty. "Shit, you need about a hundred fishes."

I snicker and nod. "What are the horses' names?"

"The big one here is Dottie, and Freckles here will be taking care of you." I raise a brow. "I know," he says, "if we run into anyone we will be sure not to mention their names."

"Agreed."

"Well, you can thank Allie Gallaway when you meet her."

"Allie?"

"The only progeny of Benjamin and Catherine. She is fifteen and has a bit of spit on her lip, real sharp tongue, so watch her. She is a reader; reminds me of you back when we were kids."

"She sounds like a challenge. You think we could spend the afternoon at the lake?" Ezra looks me up and down, assessing my body again. "Hey, I made it out here to this rock," I carp.

"Yes, a day at the lake would be a good break. Besides, Dottie and Freckles here need a good drink."

"Dottie and Freckles," I chuckle.

The next morning I am officially introduced to my ride.

"Okay, Freckles," I say as Ezra helps lift me to her saddle, "no funny business." I rub her neck. She neighs, seemingly unsympathetic to my plight. "Well, at least I weigh almost nothing. Look just there." I point to Ezra's muscular frame. "It could be much worse." She cranes her head toward me, not comprehending a word babbling from me, of course, but still I feel judged.

"Freckles is a gentle mare," says Ezra. "Your worries are misplaced. Besides, Allie vouched for her."

"Oh good," I say, unconvinced.

By afternoon we are traveling at less than a trot. I am exhausted. At least an hour ago I had resigned myself to lie along Freckles's neck. If she has taken issue with my closeness, it is missed by me.

"Halfway there," Ezra says over his shoulder.

"I cannot make it," I say as he turns to me. I feel at any moment my rump will slide from the saddle. We stop. Ezra situates me better, and then points to a thick of trees.

"I had hoped to make this just a day trip, but we can stay there for the night and pick it up again in the morning."

I nod. I am beyond tired. Sick tired. My good humor

from the day before has lifted from me.

"Sorry, Ezra," I say.

"No, I planned for this too. We have enough provisions for a few days if needed. But I would like to have you at the farm as soon as possible."

Freckles follows Ezra and Dottie to the aforementioned trees. I fade in and out of sleep. Ezra does not bother to guide me to the ground, but rather pulls me from the saddle and carries me to a blanket he has sprawled out for me. My pride would have been tarnished any other day, but this day's toll has been like nothing I have felt. As my boney body settles atop the blanket, I hear the crunch of stringy grass giving underneath me. A moment later Ezra lays a blanket upon me. I do not feel like laughing now. I turn my head with shut eyes and fall into oblivion.

August 1854
Eli, Age 17

I know this smell. A lavender cloud thick and waxy fills my chest with every breath. I find myself in Cora's family room surrounded by dozens of lighted lavender-scented candles. I focus on the flame closest to me. As the melting wax spills over the brim of the candle, I am rendered another potent wave of this breathtaking scent.

I sit in a chair and peer through Cora's hall and into Emily's room as before. I sense uneasiness beyond the thick air that surrounds me. I watch as Cora spoons tonic into her sister's mouth. Emily coughs, holding her hand toward

Cora, refusing the following dosage. My sweetheart leans toward her sister. I should not be able to hear their whispers, but I do; however, I cannot seem to decipher their secret language. I grow increasingly startled as I realize my wrists are bound to the arms of my chair. Their whispers grow to a sinister hiss so loud I begin to lose myself within them.

I try to look away, but my gaze is held toward these—these creatures I once knew. This is not Cora. Emily discovers my wide-open hiding place. With a treacherous scowl, chiseled deep within her, she wields the devil's reckoning. I shudder, bound and breathless, as her tiny index finger rises from her side to judge me. I cannot escape her glare or her haunting prophetic words, "YOU ARE NEXT, MY ELI."

CHAPTER TWENTY-ONE

June 1863
Eli, Age 26

I wake with Emily's voice still weighing against my mind. I am breathing again—gasping, in fact. Rattled to my bones, I absorb my surroundings as I recommit to a world with sunshine, cool breezes, and *Ezra*. Yes, Ezra. My nerves begin to calm as I focus on him. It is late morning. I feel as if I have been out for fifteen hours. I cannot rightly recall a time when I have fallen asleep before the sun has retired, only to wake well after the rooster's crow. Ezra has readied the horses and is eager to pull foot from camp.

"You look like hell," he says to me.

"Reckon I look better than I feel."

"Home cooking will do you good then."

After several stops to rest, we arrive at the Gallaway farm late in the afternoon.

"Mister Gallaway," Ezra exclaims as he ties Dottie's reins to an allotted post. They shake hands and embrace. These are good people. Other than myself, I know of only one other Southern man that would openly share such a hardy embrace with a colored, and I pray I will be able to see him again. I would much like to thank him for raising me—flaws and all.

Ezra pulls Freckles to the steps of the porch. I slip from the saddle into his arms. Gently he allows my foot to set upon a thick tuft of grass. Without separating from me, he hands me my staff and helps situate it along my side. As I try to hold my weight, I feel thoroughly depleted again. My leg begins to wobble as I corral every scrap of strength within me, but despite Ezra's assistance I start to sway. Mister Gallaway hurries toward me. He is faster than I would have expected, with his bulbous frame. One of his hands grips mine as the other pushes firmly upon my shoulder, allowing me to stay upright. I am embarrassed.

"Eli West," I pant, as he moves my hand up and down.

"Yes, Eli, my wife Catherine has been cooking for you. Welcome." He has a gentle demeanor about him. Normally I can accept hospitality, but in my weakened state, my heightened appreciation for his kindness seems overwhelming. "Whoa, Eli, you okay?" he says. I am not, but I nod, and collect myself. Mister Gallaway releases me after a shared glance with Ezra. Shortly I find myself, with Ezra's help, before the first porch step. I turn to him with apprehension in my eyes. Subtly I shake my head. *Impossible*, I think to myself.

"Ready?" he says.

"No," I say. They both laugh at me. I feel pitied. Ezra holds my side and presses my hip against his as he walks me up the steps. The top of my foot bounces from the lip of each step. It would be difficult to quantify the amount of shame coursing through me right now.

I find their home to be modest in most respects, but it is clear they are not without. We pass the kitchen where I see a handsome woman maybe ten years my senior cutting vegetables. She stops abruptly, setting the knife aside, and walks toward us with a welcoming smile. I am pained as our eyes meet. I try to express a simple pleasantry, but it seems I have not even that to muster. Her beautiful smile gives to her trembling hand as it meets her lips. I am a walking dead man. She reaches for her husband, and as I look away, he turns to her with comforting eyes.

I wake to an open curtain and a menacing morning sun. My hand shades my eyes as I mumble with considerable discontent. With an unsteady mind, I grasp for my bearings. Slowly my eyes adjust to the shadow cast by my frail forearm, and in this tempered light I am truly blessed by a vision. In a chair sits a girl in simple dress. Her back is straight, and her mind is enraptured by a book coddled within her delicate hands. My blurry vision soaks her in as I watch her eyes dance cross the page.

"Cora . . ." I mutter. Abruptly our eyes meet. Her body jolts from the chair.

"Oh, you are up." She smiles slightly. My arm is still protecting me from the harsh light. "I can fix this," she says, as she turns and snaps the curtains shut. My arm falls along my side. As she approaches me again, I realize my mistake.

"Thank you," I say weakly.

"The name is Allie."

I nod.

"Do you need anything, Mister West?"

"Water, please."

"Yes, just here," she points to a table near the bed as she scoops up a mug and sets it in my hand. "No, both, please; cup it with both hands."

Although I am sipping with just the one, and feel like I am managing fine, she still keeps a hand on it. I like her already.

"I have it," I say.

"I will be the judge of that, Mister West. It is me that must change the bedding if it happens to slip. Besides, we just met. How do I know if you are trustworthy?"

I smile. "What are you reading?"

"*The Life and Adventures of Nicholas Nickleby.* Dickens."

"Ezra said you were a reader."

"What else has he said?"

"That you like picking horse names."

"My Dottie and Freckles?" she asks. I nod mockingly. "Well, I was a kid when I crowned them with those names."

"You are all grown up now?"

"Enough, I suppose."

"I remember feeling that way too. Sometimes life has a funny way of turning out."

"It looks like you have had it right tough," she says, concerned. "But I do not believe my life will have half your undoings."

"For your sake I hope not, but how can you be so sure?"

"Is it not obvious, Mister West? I am pretty," she says as she flaps her lashes and purses her lips.

"Do not be surprised if later in life you discover *pretty* and *trouble* are synonyms."

After a few days I am well-accustomed to a routine. Several times a day Ezra guides me to the water closet while Missus Gallaway and Allie change the bedding and fluff the pillows if needed. I am well cared for and am gaining strength. However, I am still hampered to no end by even a simple task such as sitting up or performing a mild stretch. But I am happier; very much so, in fact. No longer am I some filthy vagabond rotting in the woods. And with this new outlook, lately, I find myself wondering if I will ever be able to repay my debt to this family with anything more than gratitude.

Allie reads to me for hours on end. And although I fall in and out of the narrative, it is her steady voice—aged beyond its years, throaty and mature, yet soothing like the siren's song—that brings me back.

"I am done for today," she says as she snaps Nickleby shut. "I want to hear your voice for a change."

"How old are you, Allie? Thirteen, fourteen?" I ask breathily. Although I have done basically nothing but digest lunch, I am dragged out.

"I will have you know, Mister West, I am well into the fifteenth year of my life, but do not be fooled. I am in possession of experience well beyond my years." I adore her wit and hope she is referring to her extensive book collection. "And, in turn, may I ask of your years?"

"Well, it would be only fair."

"It would seem."

"So ask me," I say.

"*Your* years, Mister West?"

"Let us put your endowed fifteen years to a test. Impart your best guess. And I told you, it is Eli."

"This is not fair play. I am at a disadvantage with you in your present state," she says as her eyes study me. But after further inspection, with a finger pressed against a wry smile and a squint in her eyes, she says, "thirty-seven?"

I choke. "*Really*, thirty-seven? You think I was born in 1826?"

"Well, I do not . . . you told me to guess, so I did."

"Sweetie, keep reading."

"I know, I am *only* fifteen." She sulks quietly.

"No, now do not do that. No need to be downtrodden. Trust your judgments," I say, but she continues to sulk. "Do me a favor and fetch a mirror. I would like to show you something."

At once she retrieves a small hand mirror from the washroom and places it in my waiting palm. As I stare into it, I am surprised by a familiar face. The man in the lake has followed me here and taken refuge in this silver-plated glass. I am relieved to see that he has yet to drown. He is sicker than last we met, but I am happy to see him. I think maybe he too feels some joy in knowing I am okay, or at least that I am still alive.

I ask Allie to sit next to me so that I may show her this man. The bed sags as she adjusts herself.

"You see the man beyond this glass?" I ask.

"Yes."

"I take back what I said about you needing a few more years experience. Looking at him, I think thirty-seven was generous." I place the mirror down on my blanketed chest and turn to her. "Twenty-six," I say, humbled.

Her eyes follow the furrows of my face as she touches my jaw with her tender fingertips. Her warmth wakes my flesh. Her eyes relax on mine.

"I see you now," she says, "you *are* twenty-six."

Ezra was right. I do need to watch this one's tongue.

CHAPTER TWENTY-TWO

July 1863
Eli, Age 26

Within the last couple weeks my color has been coming back. I am stronger, though my weight is still severely deficient. Missus Gallaway's beef stew is my saving grace.

This morning I sit upright with my legs dangling off the edge of the bed. I manage to secure my staff and bank it against a knot in the floor. To think I am able to lift myself is a ridiculous notion. But still, I summon my strength and attempt to heave myself from the bed. In doing so, I accomplish nothing but dizziness and a lot of heavy breathing.

"Oh, Eli!" Allie's mother gasps.

"I am okay, Catherine. Feeling righter this morning than I can remember last. If I may, I would like to join everyone for breakfast."

"Let me fetch Ezra."

"No, Cath—" But she is gone.

I wedge the staff once more against the knotted floor. My body tenses, but again, nothing happens except a renewed slight disappointment. A delicate giggle tickles my ears.

"Allie, come in, dear, and help an old man out." She enters the room with a cruel smile. "Yes, I know, I am about as entertaining as a traveling freak show—think you can help me to the breakfast table?"

"Really?"

"Hurry, your mother called for Ezra. He will not want me out of bed yet, but if you can help get this arse of mine in a breakfast chair, I bet he would make less of a fuss."

She reaches for me.

"Wait, you remember how Ezra does it, right?"

"I watch him do it three times a day. I think I can manage you. I have all this time, have I not?"

"Yes, I suppose so. It is just that I do not wish to fall. I—" Suddenly this does not feel like one of my brighter ideas. Recently, they seem to be in short supply. "Maybe I should wait for Ezra."

"Nonsense, you just said—"

"I know, but—"

"Eli," she says cocksure and determined, "remember I have fifteen years' experience. I am confident in my ability to escort you to the breakfast table. Just think of the fixings waiting for you; allow me do the rest." She sits on my left side, guides my hand around her shoulder and wraps her arm around my waist. Our bodies press against each other as if we were stitched together. A shiver runs through me as her warmth seeps into my lonely flesh. "When I say, we will both stand as one."

"You got me, right? I will not be too heavy?"

"You weigh about as much as an underwater frog fart racing its way up to the surface. I am strong. Now have *trust* in me."

"Where has your sweet tongue gone, child?"

"Sometimes the pleasures of the sweet are at the expense of the mirth. Ready?"

"N—" I say, but she is already on the rise, and I follow as I hold her shoulder tightly. She is no Ezra, but she holds me steady enough. I place my staff, and then turn to her. "You smell better than Ezra."

"I should hope so. Are you ready to take that first step?"

"Promise you have me?"

"I have quite a grasp on your boney hip here. You can feel my hand there?"

"Yes."

"Okay, move with me." I wish I could say that I help much, but it is nearly all her doing. Within moments I can see the breakfast table, however. It is dressed with everything from buttermilk eggs to crackling bacon, pork sausage, and fresh bread.

Ezra and Catherine discover Allie and myself well tangled. It must be quite a sight. Frankly, I am spent and ready to sit down as I do my best to hold my own within her grasp.

"Ezra, I am having breakfast with everyone. I refuse to go back to that bed before I have some of these fine doings."

"Well, I would hate to waste your effort. Allie, let me help set him down in a chair."

"Wait," I say. "She has me this far, let her finish." I turn toward her. "That is, if you are up for the challenge?" She nods with an air of grit and guts as she sets me down gently. A plate is set in front of me and shortly all are seated, including Allie's father.

"Benjamin," I say, "I have said this while wallowing in your spare bed, but I must say it again. I thank you for taking me into your home. You have a beautiful and generous family, but I fear I may never be able to repay my debt to you."

"Your debt is paid. Ezra has been a godsend. I had been putting certain repairs off for months, but with him, they are all nearly done. So, I may be in your debt. In fact, anytime you find yourself shot and in need of recovery, you will have a place in my home."

"Shot again? Well, that will depend on Ezra's mood."

With a smirk I place a fresh bun on my plate and bank a heap of eggs against it. I feel like I am coming back. Like I might have a chance. I look to my left to see Allie beaming as she butters a piece of bread. Ezra catches my eye. He seems happy that I have joined the family, but his eyes are telling and measuring. If my recovery continues at this rate,

DREAMS OF ELI

I know we will be leaving soon. I turn to Allie again; this time she is smiling at me. My heart breaks. I know this smile.

Late morning falls into the afternoon, and I am bedded again. With closed eyes, I am completely enchanted by Allie's storytelling. Just as powerful, though, is the silence that pervades as her voice suddenly trails off. The magic is dispelled as I open my eyes. She is preoccupied with the sunken area of the blanket where my leg should be.

"Something you would like to ask me?"

"No, nothing," she says hesitantly as she plops her nose back into *Nicholas Nickleby*. Her honey voice fills the room again. "I want to touch it," she blurts as she snaps the book shut. "Can I touch it?" she asks, tempering her demanding demeanor.

"Allie, I do not think . . ." Gently her bottom rises from her chair as she sets our story aside. With her eager eyes and childish wonder, I have a difficult time saying no. I am frankly surprised she had not asked sooner. Almost daily she witnesses Ezra's routine of unraveling the bandages and pressing only the most painful areas of the wound.

Her delicate fingers slowly begin to roll up her dress to just below her knees as she kneels down on the floor, next to my covered leg. I am not comfortable with this situation, but I do not stop her. She lifts the blankets and pushes them to the other side. I stare down at her. She reaches for the fabric covering the stump but stops just before her hand touches the bandages. She seems to ask me with her eyes that she may continue. I do not shake my head. Delicately, I feel her unraveling me. Before long, coolness caresses my healing scars.

She is awestruck as the tips of her fingers meet the scarring tissue. I feel exposed. Am I an invalid in her eyes? A show? The warmth of her tiny palm cups the severed end. I shudder. I feel pressure and only a hint of pain.

"It is called the Circular Flap Method—no bone exposure," I say, not sure if she has any idea or interest in the specifics of the procedure. The warmth of both her hands penetrates deep into the bone. I close my eyes, but immediately they snap back open as her fingers follow up my thigh, and disappear under my blankets. My hand halts her curious desire.

"No, darling." Her hands fall limp as she pulls from me. Sharply she turns away as her petite arms defiantly fold under her bosom. A forlorn silence fills the room, and as she walks from me, I hear only the scratching of her dress as it rubs against her body. "Wait," I say. "Allie . . ." She stops with her back to me, but tilts her head as her fingers begin to wipe tears.

"Is it because I am not pretty enough?" she whispers. "I have been pretending to be something I know I am not. I know that I am ugly."

Such purity; how, I ponder, how wonderful it must be to be fifteen.

"Allie, I believe of all the time we have spent together, my ears have just heard the first fib to have fallen from your lips."

"But I have been lying to you this entire time. I only wear my smile to hide my true self." Her shoulders fall forward as she further sinks into herself.

"My dear, please turn around so I may see this ugliness." After a moment she wipes her eyes again and reluctantly turns to face me.

"Oh, hmmm," I say, as I scrutinize her. "Yes, maybe." Her jaw slacks, and I smile. "Sit here," I say as I scoot over and cover my leg again. She situates herself, but seems mindful not to allow even her dress to flow against me. "Allie, do you know why we cannot be together?" She answers me with a sniffle. "It is because I am taken."

A breath is quick to fill her lungs. "But . . . never mind," she sighs.

"Please tell me."

"I was going to say something awful," she says ashamed.

"I would like to hear it. I am tough enough to take it, you know? I have half a leg gone, a mess of a mouth, half a big toe, and I am *still* here." I reach for her hand, but she pulls away and clasps both hands upon her lap. "I can take it. I promise whatever you have to say will not bring me closer to my death."

"Why do you still wear your wedding ring?"

"If I am no longer bonded by marriage?"

She seems shameful as she nods. "I thought since it was so long ago, well, I thought . . ." She looks away as her fingertips try to manage her tears.

"I still bear this ring because it holds a promise I made to someone that is very dear to me. The earthly vows I professed have met their end; however, in my heart, I have yet to let go of my promise. I carry this ring to remind me of the hope that I may one day see my love again. In my heart I believe that she is waiting for me. So I cannot return your love. At least not the love you wish. I have none to give." She sighs with sorrowed eyes. "Hand me your mirror again." She lifts it from the side table and sets it within my waiting hand. "Tell me what you see," I ask as she looks at her reflection.

"I see someone that pretends."

"What is she pretending?"

"To be pretty."

"This is what you see? Are we looking at the same person? You know, Allie, if I felt you were ugly, I would tell you."

She smirks, "No, you would not." Her shoulder bumps me and for a moment her pouting lips smile.

"Oh, yes, I would. And believe me, I have seen some ugly in my day. Do you know what I thought the day I woke up and saw you sitting in that chair?"

"No."

"I thought I had died only to wake in Heaven, and before me sat my Cora with a book in hand, just waiting for me to stir."

"You must have been disappointed."

"I think you are missing the point. I mistook you for the most beautiful, most loving angel I have ever known. Do you think if you possessed even a splinter of this *ugliness* you speak of that I would make such a preposterous mistake?"

"Well, Eli, you were pretty out of it . . ." We both laugh, and she nudges me again. "Thank you for trying to cheer me up."

"God as my witness I tell the truth." I am quiet for a moment as she dries up what is left of her tears. Her blue eyes are shining. "May I tell you a secret?" She nods as she nibbles at her bottom lip. "Allie, a boy will one day fall for you so deeply he will not know which way is up. I know this just as I know the sun will rise a thousand years from now."

"How can you be sure?"

"Now for the secret—it is kindness, not fairness of skin, that will enchant this boy. Sure, he will fall for your darling eyes and the warmth of your touch, but he will *love* you for your kindness."

"But, how do you know this?" she queries me again.

"Because I have received and lived within the light of this kindness. And this kindness I speak of, no man is able to resist it." Slowly she pulls the mirror from my hand, sets it upon her lap, and turns to me.

"I would like to believe Cora and I could have been friends. Do you think she would have liked me much?"

"She would have loved you."

CHAPTER TWENTY-THREE

August 1863
Eli, Age 26

My recovery is well on its way, as are the days. Four more weeks have past. We have been on the farm for six weeks. I wake with Ezra at my side, and there is a peace about him that calms me. In a single motion I sit up, draw in a deep breath, and stretch my wiry arms above me.

"No need to strain yourself," he says.

"I am not. Just doing better."

"I have been watching your progress. Looks like some weight has come back. I have been meaning to check on you with more regularity, but lately, I have been mending the east fence." He wipes his brow with a calloused palm. "It has been tough going."

"Let me know if you need any help," I say as we trade smiles. "Allie has been filling in, so there is no need to fret about me."

"And what about Benjamin's gift?"

"The wheeled trap of death from 1820?" I say as I gesture toward a dilapidated wheelchair.

"That would be the gift I speak of."

"Allie coerced me into it with a verbal promissory note of a glass of Apple Jack. She can be persuasive."

"Indeed, she can be. Be easy on the brandy."

"I had just the one while she pushed me about the farm. Quite the sweet afternoon cap, I must say."

"Yes, I saw that. Seems like you two were having a good ol' time."

"It was mostly the Jack, and I did not want to disappoint Benjamin after all the trouble he went to." I notice a tenor of obligation trailing my words like I am being put upon. For some reason I do not want Ezra to know I have been having a wonderful time while Allie wheels me around. The open breeze and the unencumbered sunshine that splashes across my face have felt like a blessing.

"Should I ask Benjamin to barter the chair for something else?"

"No," I say quickly. "Perhaps I should continue with it. The outings seem to keep Allie in high spirits, so for her sake—"

"Okay, for Allie then," he says, humoring me. "How long can you stand on your own?"

"About three minutes. Allie still guides me back to the

bed, but I think soon I will be able to handle that too."

"Good," he says as he examines my leg. "So, it seems Allie is less than shy around you, huh?" I am sheepish and cannot help but look away. "Hmm, yes, I see. Well, you need to tell her." I hear his words but refuse to speak. "You should tell her."

"Yes, I know."

"Soon, Eli."

"I will . . . today at the pond."

Allie fluffs a pillow as my mind drifts.

"What are you thinking about?" she asks. "Looks mighty involving from where I stand."

"What would you say about pushing my bones down to the pond today?"

"I would love to," she says, as she wedges the pillow behind me. "We could picnic! Mother has a few flapjacks left from breakfast, and I think we have a half jar of apple butter. It would make for a fine early lunch. Oh, this will be *some pumpkins!*"

"Any peanut brittle left?"

"Yes, but what about your mouth?"

"I just like the way it melts against my tongue, but if you are that concerned I will try to keep the biting to a minimum. How about some cookies too?" Her hands meet her hips. "What?" I say. "You heard Ezra's orders. Am I not trying to fatten up? It is tough goings in this life. Step lively now."

Benjamin's beaten chair creaks and sways as Allie negotiates the pocked trail. I sway to the left after a particularly treacherous chasm—no less deep than three fingers of whiskey—staggers the contraption. She is sure to correct its path, but I fear another jostle like that may loose a wheel, and me along with it.

As we approach the pond, the breeze reminds me of home. Abruptly, she jolts the chair to a stop at the water's edge of the deck. Our lunch basket lurches forward from my lap. She gasps, but I am quick to grab it.

"You have it?" she asks.

"Do you think I would chance my brittle to the fishes?"

"You and your sweets."

The water with its glassy sheen seems to beg for my participation, but I am in no mood for a swim.

"Do you think I could wade my feet for a while?" I say, gesturing toward the water. "I mean my foot."

"Sure."

I push myself from the chair. Her arms are ready to catch me in case I decide to pick a quarrel with balance today.

"You have it," she says as she gently touches my shoulder. I am nearly convinced by her encouragement, but I begin to falter.

"Okay, I need you—*more* of you," I say with slight desperation. I welcome the fullness of her warm hug as it steels my confidence. Slowly, we ease our bottoms to the planks below. The uneven boards hurt my boney rump as I scoot to the end of the deck. Allie plucks off her slippers, sets them aside, and sits close to me. My bare foot dangles ankle deep while my other leg hovers well over the surface.

"Oooww, chilly!"

"Give it a moment," I say.

She crowds closer, firmly pressing our thighs together. The width of the deck just barely accommodates us. We talk little as her toes fiddle with my foot. I look to my left into the deep and am startled to see the man in the lake again. He seems happier. His gaunt body also seems stronger than last I saw him. I smile with him, and then raise my face to the sky. As Allie and I listen to the melodies hidden within the trees above, a cantankerous fish is spit from the water's surface and splashes back in.

"Should have been a bird," I say, expecting a giggle from her. Instead, I discover sadness as her eyes meet mine.

"Perhaps my water-breathing friend knows she is trying to be something she is not." She turns away from me.

"Allie? I—" My voice falls upon her delicate neckline.

"I know why you have asked me here today. Please,

Eli, allow me to pretend a little while longer. For my sake, keep your words." She turns her head back to me, a solemn expression adorning such a beautiful face.

She reaches for our basket and breaks off pieces of peanut brittle. Her trembling hand shares a small piece with me.

"Allie—" Before I am allowed to continue, I feel her arms wrap around my waist. She pulls me closer still. Gently, I try to turn away, but her soft lips meet mine.

An innocent kiss. And as she pulls away, my ear is met with a whisper. "You have no more love to give, but I am unable to trammel love. No matter what I do, I cannot seem to keep it from flowing. I know you will be leaving soon. I pray that you will not forget our time together."

I should say something—anything—but I do not. I just hold her hand, and then I let her go.

Soon, we are well into flapjacks and apple butter. And before I know it, I am back in my chair listening to the rhythmic patter of the wheels rolling across planks.

I press my palms against the wheels, halting the contraption as we meet the pocked trail again. With the trees swaying above and the golden light showering down upon us, I look up to see a perplexed young lady.

"Is something wrong?" she says. For a moment nothing is said as I stare into hurt tender eyes.

"Allie, thank you." The corners of her mouth curl just slightly upward as she pushes forward, and I sink back into my well-worn creaky leather-backed wheelchair.

CHAPTER TWENTY-FOUR

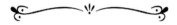

September 1863
Eli, Age 26

I am well in need of rest as I lean against the trunk of a magnolia tree. Ezra relieves Freckles and Dottie of our provisions. My debt to the Gallaway house still weighs on me. Ezra tells me not to worry about the supplies and lent horses. He has agreed to settle our debt whenever they are in need of his services. But I do worry.

My left leg aches, largely because it has a rusty iron frame buckled tightly around it. A wooden right foot, gnarled and unkempt by its prior owner, is biscuit jointed and screwed to the unforgiving metal. I suppose it is better to be able to walk—albeit in circles now that I have two right feet—rather than having to be carried around by Ezra. I understand why Benjamin traded the rickety chair for the leg brace: wheelchairs do not carry well on horses. Admittedly, I had taken a liking to the creaky old thing.

We could have gone the less strenuous path of pulling

a carriage and traveling the main roads, but where there are worn roads there are usually many people. The fewer conversations we have with strangers the better. Being in these backwoods, however, does not mean I am free from apprehension. God forbid if we were to cross paths with my brothers in arms. No doubt I would be reinstated and eventually discharged from the army, but the fuss involved could prove fatal to me.

And as for Ezra, his fate would be well beyond my influence. He might be shot dead, or he being more than able-bodied, he might be shackled and sold. Perhaps because of his brawn, he would be unofficially conscripted into the fray, to fight for the South with little more than his bare hands.

Pondering such dreary potentials brings me unease. I stare at my caged leg, and then unfasten the top two buttons of Benjamin's sweaty shirt. A few weeks back, Ezra and I were downright dapper in our boiled shirts. But after several weeks of lathered horses and Mississippi clime we are soiled.

Despite my discomfort, I believe the circuitous route to Jackson is best. I count twenty-one days since we have left Allie's farm, and four days since we have seen anyone but ourselves. For every day that passes that we do not encounter an unfamiliar soul, I am grateful.

I unbuckle the leather straps, and then pitch the iron prison to my left. It clanks and pings as it tumbles away from me. I half hope it would throw a screw, or snap altogether. As I massage my leg I wince at bruises and skin gnawed raw from Freckles's rhythmic trot.

"Check her left flank," I say to Ezra. "I am mangled badly by the contraption. She may need some attention." He nods and runs his hands across her side.

"Seems fine. Does not look like the contraption penetrated through your trousers."

"Just me then," I say half disappointed. I do not want to see the beast hurt. But it humbles me to realize that it would have been soothing for me to share a little of my misery.

An infection encumbers the remainder of my big toe. It weakens me with each day that passes. When I remove my boot I can smell that same death smell Ezra had warned me about back in the cave.

He manages the infection the best he can. I know him well enough to know he is holding a truth from me. I can sense his eagerness to separate me from my agony, but it seems he will not broach the subject until, perhaps, we are home in Jackson.

I rub in salve from Ezra's satchel. Instead of my asking for it several times a day, he has allowed me to keep it. Not much good it does though. It lessens the acute pain, but I fear my sickness is down to the bone. The thought of losing this foot too is more than I wish to consider, especially so far from home. I only hope I can make it to my own bed before Ezra shares his secret with me.

For several nights now during the cool evening hours a cough stirs, and when it gets going I cannot rightly stop the hacking. Whiskey helps.

Along with the menacing cough, it seems the Virginia Quickstep has caught up with me too. This concerns Ezra the most, and rightly so; dysentery has killed more of my brothers than muzzle metal.

I imagine the man in the lake would bend my ear with a few choice words. Perhaps I would bend his too. I close my eyes to the forest, and as I do, Ezra's footsteps fade and my mind drifts. I am back at the pond with Allie. We are hip to hip with our bottoms against the uneven planks. She smiles with me as our three feet dangle in the cool water. I turn from her and peer into the reflective surface and see my friend staring back at me. He appears concerned for my well-being. I, however, do not reflect his apprehension. Before me is a strong and virile man. His worry for me bleeds away, only to sharpen into a judgmental glare. I envy his recovery. As I examine him, ugliness cankers my guts. I should be happy for him, but I am not. His eyes scream at me as his lips silently mouth one word: "EAT!"

"I AM!" I bark into the forest as I jolt awake. For a moment I am lost. I look for the man in the lake but find nothing but twigs, dirt and Ezra. He has cleared a small pit and started a fire.

"Who are you talking to?" he says, as his blade pierces a hole in a can of Van Camp beans.

"Nobody you know," I say, grumpy as a molested rattlesnake. To my left, my hand rests on a knapsack.

"I thought you might want that close to you tonight." I roll the sack down to find a half bottle of drink and Dickens's *Nicholas Nickleby*.

"Allie," I whisper, as my fingers trace the binding. I did do my best to refuse this gift. "I have my own copy. You keep this one," I recall saying to her as she placed the book in my hands. "*Look beyond the pages*," she said during her teary good-bye. I open the story. "*Look beyond the pages*," I whisper while leafing through several worn pages. It dawns on me while still in my sleepy stupor, it is our shared memories, our time together, that is her gift to me. These words are simply a token gesture, a reminder of . . . us.

I look toward Ezra's powerful forearms as he stirs the pot of beans. "You must not think much of me," I say, as I raise the spine of the book to my lips.

"Befriending a pretty girl makes me think less of you? Now, me helping with your *necessaries* is a different story . . ." I do not laugh as I feel my stomach churn.

"I did a great disservice to that girl. She was a selfish distraction for me, and she is owed more than that."

"Distraction? Did you . . ."

"What? No. Never."

"I am not your judgment," he says defensively. "You two seemed to be quite close. In a short time she would make for a lovely wife." I pucker toward him, nearly in a fit. My fingertips turn my wedding ring as I feel the intrusion of his meddling. He continues to stir. "Eli, do you love her?" My blood blisters as I absorb his query. I am barely able to hold my tongue, but after I simmer some, my contempt crumbles into a shame so deep I am silenced.

I have been hiding from myself. I have been fooling no one. Allie and I are more than friends, and in admitting this to myself, I must too admit that I have committed the gravest betrayal.

"Do you love her?" he asks again. "Do you wish to go

back to her—back to the farm?" I thoughtfully rummage through a few more pages, and then close the book, tucking it deep into the folds of the sack.

"No," I say steely eyed. "And no, I do not wish to go back."

CHAPTER TWENTY-FIVE

September 1863
Eli, Age 26

W e will need to cook both of these tonight," Ezra says, as he holds two ducks by their limp necks. "You want to help?" He hands me a bird. I begin to pluck the feathers as I lean against a rock. The stars are beginning to show, and a cold breeze roughs my neck. Ezra pokes at our fire, spreading the embers about. The warmth is welcome. I feel it blush across my face.

After a while both the birds are gutted and spitted. I hand him mine, and he steadies them over the fire.

I sit with my eyes closed, listening to the woods and the crackling of duck grease.

"Did I ever tell you about a chasm back west?" Ezra asks. It seems he is going to tell me regardless of my answer.

"Nope," I say with a cracked eyelid.

"How far you suppose the Gallaway farm is from home?"

"In my current situation, reckon, weeks. Five days if we pull foot."

"No, the distance," he says.

"Hmm, hundred miles?"

"Feels 'bout right. I wish you could see this canyon. We could ride along its belly the distance it takes us to ride from Benjamin's to your father's beaten porch steps, and back again and still not reach its end."

"That is a hell of a hole."

"Eli, this is more than a hole. Nothing but God's will could carve a chasm this deep. I do not frighten easily, but I must confess, some nights I could not wait for the light."

"Where is it?"

"It feels like a lifetime away. Travel west through Texas and then well into the Indian territory."

"When were you there?"

"Summer of '55. It would have been just before I wrote you from California. Wish we could have traveled together."

"1855? Cora and I had just wed that February," I say with happiness in my heart. "And by June, I was rubbing her bulbous belly, and September, well . . ."

"I did not mean—"

"No, I just meant to say at the time I was better suited in Jackson."

Ezra drops his head for a moment and turns the birds. "I had a girl for a time. Did I ever write about that?"

"No, I just received the one letter. I remember reading that it would be the one and only."

"I remember that. I would have liked to have told you about her, but at the time of that writing, her departure had still haunted me. Although our time together was brief, it was the closest thing I have ever had to a normal life."

"How did you meet?"

"I removed a ball from her brother's shoulder. She was a savage."

I raise an eyebrow. "Savage? Really?"

"Her tribe was grateful, and for a time, I had become known as a healer. I learned many remedies from them. You may have felt the spins after eating in the cave. That was from one of their concoctions. Sorry for the headaches if you suffered them. That particular remedy often strikes a fit of head pain."

I wave, gesturing my acceptance. "What was her name?"

"Aiyana. She told me it was neither Apache nor Cherokee, the tribes of her father and mother, but from a far-off land."

"What does it mean?"

"I wish I knew. She may have told me at some point, but I never fully learned her language, although I tried desperately. And most of what I had learned is lost on me now."

"Did you break her heart?" My words are quick and thoughtless.

"It would seem that our fates are closely tangled. She was taken away from me. Or I suppose I was taken from her," he says pensively. "We were fast asleep one evening. Being unmarried, we had not yet been blessed to share the night, but this did not stop her from seeking me. One particular evening, however, a dozen white men on horseback pillaged the village. Many were killed, and most of the grass huts were quick to catch their fire.

"As I stared into her eyes, fear told me this was to be the last night we would see each other. I kissed her, determined to not allow that to be. I clutched my pistol and headed into the fray. Already several villagers were left for dead, bleeding from revolver and rifle shots.

"When I came upon Aiyana's brother, he had been shot again, but this time in the lower belly. I plunged my finger into him as I tried to retrieve the metal, but he stopped me and cried out for his sister. He grabbed my arm with bloody hands and pointed toward a path in the woods. I nodded and went back to my hut where I found her frozen like wintered stone.

"'We must go into the woods,' I said, as I pointed where her brother had directed me. I flanked her as we ran through the carnage. I shot at one of the horsemen, but among the screams and protecting her, I was too distracted and missed. The horseman's sword slashed my shoulder, but the blade did not cut through the bone. My second shot hit the horseman's lower back as he galloped past us. Upon his return to finish me, he slumped off the saddle and hit the ground like a smith's hammer to an anvil.

"I grabbed Aiyana by the wrist and flung her tiny body on the back of the horse. With haste I followed, and within moments we were beyond the edges of the village. We must have ridden for half the night. I did not know where she was guiding me, but she seemed to know the way. We were lucky to have the moon that night. I do not need to remind you of the dangers of traveling in darkened wood."

"What about the split flesh?" I ask.

"It was not in dire need of a dressing. As we continued, I felt her pat my leg. I was not inclined to stop, but she insisted. I do not remember what was said, but she was clear that she wanted off that horse. I helped her down. Her skin was yellow in the moonlight. I think you would have liked her. She had Cora's sass."

I slowly nod.

He continues, "She released the horse's reins from my palm, caressed its flank and neck, and gently guided it away from us. 'No,' I argued, but the look in her eyes convinced me. It trotted away, blankets, ropes, saddle, and all. She held my hand as she looked up at me. With her other hand she pointed toward the horse's direction, then rubbed my chest and hers, and then sniffed her palm. 'Goshe,' she said, and then yelped in my face like an animal.

"'Dogs?' I questioned. She did not seem to know what to say, so she barked and howled into the night. To this day, I am still unsure of exactly what 'goshe' means, but I think a dog, coyote, wolf, or some other trail-sniffing beast is close. None of which I wanted to meet that night.

"However, at the time, I did not like it. Shooing the horse, I felt was a mistake. After all, they are able to run for hours and at such a greater pace than dogs with their master afoot. But these were her lands, her tribe had taught me much, so I followed her faithfully.

"A hundred feet from where the horse was released, she led me up a near vertical rock formation. No horse would do us any good, and for that matter, no dog, no matter how devout, could surmount such a task.

"Once we reached the top I realized the time we saved, as she pointed out the lengthy path she had originally intended. After traveling several more miles we found shelter at the edge of a meadow and rested for the night.

"We woke in each other's arms." Ezra's gaze drifts into the firelight. "The sadness in her eyes, that will never leave me. She had seen her brother dying as I rushed her through the village. That morning she wept, for hours.

"We walked for half a day, foraging along the way, and ended up in a valley fraught with abandoned huts similar to the ones we had left. I assumed this was her former village. We stayed for weeks and not once did we cross anyone—our very own Eden. We made love every night, and I know this is going to sound odd, but I think I married her."

"You do not know?" I say. "You should know."

"I *should* know." He reaches down his shirt and retrieves a knotted leather necklace. "Aiyana made this for me."

I lean forward. It appears to be braided leather with an ornate knot tied through the center. His countenance turns pensive again.

"One afternoon I came back with a rabbit in hand for supper and found a rainbow assortment of wet clays spread out in front of her. I set the kill aside as she beckoned me to sit across from her. She smeared rusty-colored clay across her fingers, and then reached for my face. Unaccustomed to the ritual, I backed away. She laughed, clasped my hand, and pulled me to her. She then placed my hand upon her heart as she began to paint my face with the assorted clays.

"Wish I could tell you what she said. It seemed like a prayer or a chant of some ilk. Her song flowed like honey from her lips. And then she smeared clay across my fingertips, and placed her hand on my chest as my other hand still laid against her chest. My painted fingertips were then guided along her face as she continued to sing her song, I assume in the same pattern as she had painted me.

"She pulled me forward so that our foreheads met. She told me that she loved me. I told her that I too loved her.

"As she pulled away from me, she sat down and placed my hand in her lap. Adjacent to her thigh sat a queer leather necklace. It had two loops and a single knot in the middle. She looped a strap over my head and handed the other loop to me as she leaned forward. I guided it over her ebony hair where it rested along the back of her neck, tethering us together.

"Her palm cradled the knot as she pulled it to her mouth, separating the knot along one side. It was nearly halved as it hung between us. Her hands guided mine to the dangling knot. I closed my fingers around it. She pushed my hands to my mouth and placed a particular piece of the knot between my teeth. I severed the string, forever breaking the knot into halves. Each side fell against our hearts. She again reached for my hand and pressed it against her chest, but this time my palm covered her half-knot. And in turn, her hand found my chest as she pressed my half-knot under her palm. The happiness that swelled my heart during these days . . ." Ezra clutches his half-knot to his chest.

"I would say you are married." I chuckle for a moment, but then hold my tongue, dreading the answer to my next question. "Where is she?"

He removes his hand from his chest and stares at me.

"Let me ask you, Eli," he says with ebbing sentimentality, "is it the burden of every white man to harm and pillage the souls of all other men that do not share his skin?"

"Not this white man," I say. But my words leave him unfulfilled.

CHAPTER TWENTY-SIX

September 1863
Eli, Age 26

One morning, I joked with Aiyana that I would follow her during her necessaries. After my fun I let her go. But by that time she was nearly bursting for a pee and darted around a rock formation. Looking back, this was a blessing. I heard the trot of horses.

"My pistol was out of reach; I had had no reason to keep it near. As far as I knew we were alone. I am not so naive theses days," he says. "We had not seen another person since the village massacre—at least a month had passed.

"Three horsemen were upon me with pistols drawn before I could react.

"'Well, look here,' one of them said. His hand shook— not a good quality in a shooter if you are looking down his barrel.

"'Good day,' I said, as I raised my palms to them. The

one in the middle had a scheming glint in his eye. He was portly, but looked like he could carry his own. The third horseman held a steady pistol as his eyes scouted beyond me.

"'You alone here?' said Portly, as they all inspected my squatter's camp.

"'Yes,' I said, hoping their eyes would not meet the rocks where Aiyana hid.

"'Yes, what?' said Portly.

"'Yes, Master,' I said as my brow furrowed. Portly relaxed some and holstered his pistol. Shaky and Steady still held me within their fire line.

"'How long you been in these parts?' Portly said, as he placed his hands on the horn of his saddle.

"'Couple days, but just passing through, really.'

"'Seems like an awful lot of stuff for just you,' he said, as he pointed to a few blankets and whatnots.

"'I plundered all the abandoned huts here, and this is the lot of it. Seemed they might have been in a hurry to get.'

"'Hmm,' he nodded. 'You feeling all right?'

"'Far as I know, why?'

"'Them Apache blankets, right? They could be fraught with the pox. Hell, any Indian wares, I would leave to the trails.'

"'He looks right to me, boss,' Shaky said. Portly did not like being interrupted as he silenced his associate with a glare.

"'Where you aiming to head?'

"'California,' I lied, not knowing that I would soon find myself in California nonetheless.

"'No kidding? Well, if that ain't a downright coincidence. Us too!' he smiled. His teeth were worse than yours.

"Steady kept his eye on me, but Shaky laughed—I knew the second they rode up that he was the weakest within the group.

"'You feel like riding with us?' Portly asked.

"'Much obliged,' I told him, 'but I would prefer to make my own way.'

"'Prefer?' he said. 'Boys, we have ourselves an educated Negro,'" Ezra says to me as he turns our ducks.

"'I reckon you should come with us,' Portly insisted.

"'But I have earned my freedom.'

"Steady, with sinister eyes, finally smiled at me.

"'Well,' Portly said, 'consider yourself reacquired.' He drew his pistol once again, and with his other hand he tossed a rusty pair of wrist shackles."

Ezra's arms bulge as he struggles with his story. I stare into the fire and listen.

"Eli, it had been years since I had heard the jangle of irons around my wrists. Mister Johnson had last shackled me when I was fifteen years old."

"What did you do about Portly?" I ask.

"Well, I had no choice it seemed. I picked up the

bracelets and locked them around my wrists. That was when Steady finally broke his silence. 'Turn around,' he said. I heard him dismount from his horse. With my back to him I looked toward the rocks where Aiyana still hid. As Steady commanded me to my knees, my eyes caught Aiyana. Those once lovely eyes glared with a fury.

"Aiyana was studying the men at my back, possibly assessing an attack strategy. But as my eyes penetrated into hers, I shook my head, hoping she would not entertain such tomfoolery. As concerned the men, as far as I knew, they had not detected my gesture.

"I heard the crush of gritstone under Steady's boots, and then felt a rap across my skull. I assumed it was a bump from a rifle butt. I woke after nightfall slumped against a rock next to a fire, similar to how we are now, but not right. I felt dumber than a ninny, like I had been drugged. My wrists burned as they had tightened the shackles, but I paid little mind to the shackles and instead, desired the cure of four and a half fingers of whiskey for my head."

"Were your legs bound as well?" I ask.

"No. Had they been, I might not be here to tell you this story. After a moment my wits began to gather. It seemed the night was well into its hours. Of the three men only Shaky was up, and he had yet to see that I had come around.

"I do not know how, but I felt that Aiyana was near. She would not allow me to be taken. I heard a snap of a twig and beyond the firelight, I saw a tiny figure dart among the trees. After a moment Shaky stood with a hand holding his crotch. I closed my eyes and breathed evenly as he walked over to me. Convinced that I was still out, he scurried off into the night to find relief.

"Once Shaky was amid full stream, I heard the crack of his skull being staved in by the hand of my little savage. His body slumped and flopped to the ground. Then a large rock thudded against the dense soil. It was loud. Too loud I felt.

"Portly snorted from the commotion, but did not shift much. Steady, however, woke with a jerk and a start. He sat upright and gathered himself, as I again closed my eyes. I felt the silence of the woods and his stare upon me. I knew Steady would not be fooled easily. His hammer cocked as he headed about fifteen paces north. Shaky was south of us.

"I heard a distinct knock and a shower of granite tumbled down the face of a large boulder. Aiyana's signal was bold. I knew that I would have to pull foot if she was to have a chance of surviving him. Steady turned toward the falling rocks. I hoped Aiyana found a tree or something, anything that would move her out of the line of fire. It seemed that we had one thing in common: he was a killer—savage as a meat ax. I was confident, however, that he would not pursue her much beyond our camp. I would not have if I were in his position.

"Steady was out of my sight, and beyond my earshot, but I had a general idea of where he was surveying. I turned toward Portly. He hummed a snore, and as he exhaled, I pulled my chains taut to lessen the rattle of my scurry. I was able to retrieve his pistol and set it just behind him, out of reach. He had not noticed.

"His head rested awkwardly against a boulder. I wanted to dispatch him as quietly as possible, so I lay next to him, nearly scraping his pantaloons. I crushed my elbow into his sternum. His chest collapsed as his head lurched forward off the rock, accompanied by a horrified gasp. With my chained wrists quickly looped around his neck, I yanked him in close to me, tight, and began to hear the sound of cartilage cracking.

"I felt confident the crushing of his throat would incapacitate his ability to scream, not to mention his collapsed chest. However, it was any whimper or short-lived scuffle that most concerned me. As he gasped for his next breath, I crossed my forearms, and pulled my wrists down to the elbows. The iron links had nowhere to go but deeper into his blubbery neck.

"Within seconds his throat gurgled and I was covered in blood. His flaying arms and legs simmered down. Had I had sufficient time, I would have removed his head from his neck. Looking back, I was halfway there. I stopped because Steady would be upon me soon. I rolled Portly off me. His face slid down his resting rock as I retrieved his pistol. Quietly, and with a heavy breath, I rummaged through the fat man's pockets and found the shackle keys.

"I was making too much noise, but in this moment I had to remove the binding metal. The first shackle slid from my wrist like hog's grease, but the second jammed. Steady's shot shredded the night as the ball tore past my left ear. I rolled behind Portly's sleeping boulder and his body.

"'Well played,' I heard Steady say calmly.

"'I told you I have earned my freedom; do not make me earn it again with your life,' I shouted. He was at the perimeter of the fire glow, maybe twelve feet from me, but he was well-guarded by two mated tree trunks. Had it been just one, I might have had a shot.

"'Just business,' Steady said.

"'I do not wish to be your business,' I countered. 'You can take a horse and leave, and we both could put all this tomfoolery behind us.'

"'Never been known to cower to a colored. See no reason to change tonight. Seen Clemens out there just yonder. Nice work. And looks like Eddington is done for too. I may owe you a debt of gratitude. When I auction your hide, I will be the one to collect full.'"

Ezra's stomach grumbles. "Ducks looks ready," he says as he sets them away from the flame. "Leg okay?" he asks as he carves into one of them and hands some meat to me at the end of his blade. I gesture for him to continue and begin to eat.

"Where was I?" he asks as he takes a generous bite.

"Clemens and Eddington are dispatched, and he is to collect."

"Oh, right, so he tells me about Shaky, or Clemens, in the woods, but I tell him it was not my doing. In doing so, I had hoped to ferret him out of his hold."

Ezra takes another juicy bite, chews for a while, and then continues.

"'I know,' Steady said, 'I found your girl, and you are not going to like what happens next.' He risked himself by showing his shooting arm as his pistol was pointed not at me, but directly at Aiyana hidden behind a few saplings.

"She must have thought the night would have protected her. Steady cracked two shots, and Aiyana fell, but I had squeezed Portly's trigger three times in Steady's direction. With the shackle weighing my wrist, and their poisonous concoction still coursing in my veins, I missed the first shot veering wide. But the second caught his arm and as he lurched back the third pierced the bark of the tree, and the ball flanked him. He too fell. I waited for his pistol to go limp in his hand. It did.

"I called out to Aiyana. She was crying. When I crawled to her she latched on to me, shaking and cold. I had to peel her from my body. Her resistance was promising. I groped her entire body searching for blood. But I found none. Her smile came back. I lay with her for a moment as we celebrated our reunion. Did I tell you that she held my beard in her hands when we were close?"

"Sounds nice," I say.

"I walked over to Steady. He was long gone as far as I could tell. But I fetched his pistol and pressed his partner's barrel against his forehead just the same.

"Aiyana and I packed up a horse and took whatever valuables we thought might be useful. But as we saddled her, I heard the bark of a pistol cut through the night. Aiyana slumped in my arms and fell from me. I pulled Portly's gun. It was Shaky with probably the luckiest shot of his life. His staved cranium was apparently not as staved as I had hoped. In hindsight, this was my oversight. I should have made sure, but so much had happened in such a short time, and I was not yet in my right mind. I answered Shaky with two shots to his chest.

"I pulled Aiyana behind Portly's boulder. She'd been hit in the upper thigh. I tore a sleeve from Portly's shirt and secured it around her leg the best I could. Her scream is still with me."

I am morose and stop eating.

"Haste followed my boots and with caution I approached Shaky and kicked his pistol away. He was really shaking. His chest rose and fell like a humming bird's wings. As I stood above him I stared down deep into his eyes. He seemed preoccupied and within his own thoughts. I took a step and slowly pushed his neck with the sole of my boot. As I pressed, I believe he saw me, as a flicker of his life met my eyes. That was what I was waiting for. I wanted him to see me. I wanted his recognition while I crushed this life's last breath against his collapsing windpipe.

"With Shaky dispatched, I rushed back to Aiyana. In hindsight, I should not have relished my revenge—for every moment spent with Shaky, another was stolen from Aiyana. When I reached her, she too was trembling and bloody. I needed to remove the bullet, but I did not have any instruments. She bawled as I fished her leg with a finger, but I was unable to go deep enough.

"I found a chow spoon and plunged its stem into her while I held her face to the dirt. I felt I was betraying her. But I had to find it, and I needed her to be as still as possible. With blood pouring from her thigh and her screams tearing at my ears, I felt it. The ball had lodged against the bone. But I could not seem to peel it out of place.

"Knowing where to go now I tried my finger again, but it was still too thick to dislodge it. I again sank the butt end of the spoon into her flesh, and this time was able to nudge the ball. As I began to needle it to the surface, it shot out with a torrent of blood. I pressed her leg the best I could and was able to get the gush of blood down to a trickle, but it was now pooling within. I carried her to the edge of the fire pit, set the spoon into the embers, and waited. She was weak and no longer fought me. She reached for my beard but fell short of it as her arm slumped against her bosom. I kissed her.

"'I am sorry' I said to her, 'I have to stop the bleeding.' I reached for the spoon. It was now red hot at the tip and seared my hand. I knew generally where the bleed was coming from, as I was familiar with the artery. But I could not see what I was doing. As I released the pressure from her thigh, the red-hot spoon disappeared into her flesh. I swear her brother, a world away, heard his sister's wail. And then she fell silent.

"I squeezed the flesh around the spoon hoping the artery and surroundings would cauterize. Smoke seeped from her wound. The smell was sickening.

"I then jostled the spoon, hoping not to tear any new bleeds. I waited for the blood to bellow out again, but it did not, not like before. I felt for her pulse; it was weak. I set the spoon back into the fire and within a moment it was hot enough to sear the last of the trickle of blood. I secured the tourniquet again and set her upon a horse. My navigation was frantic and reckless as we made our way through the woods. I was worried that I could not hear even a whimper from her. I must have ridden two or three miles. I feared she would not make it to the morning light if we continued, so I found a spot where I could keep her warm.

"She did not wake until well into the day. After the initial shock of her condition, she calmed and drank from the canteens I had pilfered from the horsemen. I tended to her regularly, but despite this, over the next week, her leg became rife with pus. Any doctor that tells you pus has healing attributes is a fool. It is a harbinger of the worst kind.

"She was in so much pain, Eli, and I could not save her." He throws duck bones into the fire. The fat crackles and spits. "She left me in the night clasping this knot."

I say nothing for a spell. I now possibly understand his hanging on to me, and his determination to take my leg.

"Ezra, why did you come back here?"

"I did not want to at first. After what had happened I could not bear to stay in The Territory. And with Mississippi still raw, I had decided to go west into California after all. But trouble eventually caught up with me again. Nearly ran into a California collar."

"So trouble brought you home?"

"Trouble is a funny thing. My skin seems to bring it out of others, and then their trouble undoubtedly becomes my own. I would not expect you to understand."

He continues, "Trouble is not the reason why my feet walk these woods again. I came back to Mississippi, because this is the land where my family rests. This is my home. It is where one day, I will die too."

"Yes, but here in Mississippi that day may come with a quicker step. What will you do if you are recognized and associated with Johnson's death?"

"I wanted to be home. This is the soil that has touched my father's hands. This is where I must be. As for Johnson—I have grown, and the facial hair helps. I have nothing to worry about if even you cannot recognize me."

Abruptly, I raise my hand to Ezra and tilt an ear toward a stirring to my far right. Ezra heard it too. Twigs carelessly snap as something rapidly moves toward us. My hand draws my Colt and clicks the hammer back. I too hear the click of Ezra's pistol. And we wait with steady hands.

CHAPTER TWENTY-SEVEN

September 1863
Eli, Age 26

A dark figure fumbles into our camp. It is a slave girl. She winces as she falls to her hands and knees. As she turns to us, I witness a fear in her eyes so tangible it is as if the devil himself is with us.

"No, no, no, no . . ." she whispers as she attempts to back step, but drops to her rump. I place my revolver back into its holster as I turn toward Ezra with a wry smile. He is relieved, as am I. Ezra stands and walks over to the girl, raising his palms. She might be fourteen. Her wrists are shackled, and her feet are slashed and bleeding. Her wild eyes blaze toward Ezra. He takes a knee next to her but she misconstrues his kindness and curls up into herself. Ezra touches her shoulder. She flinches as she clutches at her ragged and worn maid's dress.

"Little one," he says. Nothing escapes past her lips. He retreats from her, grabs a tin of water from his belongings, and then returns to her side. She is softly panting.

I look at the other duck. It smells good.

He places his hand back on her shoulder. She shudders again, but her initial shock seems to be wearing off.

"Drink," says Ezra, as he wraps his hand around the back of the girl's neck, pulling her to the tin. The wetness washes over her cracked and weathered lips. She grabs hold and gulps as fast as her throat will allow her to swallow.

"Thank you," she says as she catches her breath. Ezra pulls her to her feet, but they are apparently too swollen and bloodied to carry her another step. He scoops the child into his arms and carries her over to the fire.

"Hi," I say gaily, which is out of character with the disquiet of the moment. "You hungry?" I ask as I point to the roasted duck. She nods. Ezra unbuttons his knife again, slices off a large piece, and hands it to her. She accepts it, graciously nodding in his direction, and then sinks her teeth into the meat like a starving wolf. Ezra cuts a juicy piece for me as well. We all eat in silence. The second duck is just as good.

"Do you want more?" Ezra asks.

"Yes, please. Thank you, Mister," she whispers, as he hands her another hunk.

"What is your name?" he asks.

"Alse," she says meekly.

"That is a pretty name," I say. "You were running pretty hard."

"Master and his dogs is coming to get me," she says as she chews a mouthful. "I ran away at first light."

"You can stay here tonight with us," says Ezra.

"No," she says sharply. "I mean to thank you, but I must keep on."

"Alse, I am not afraid of any dogs."

"But these *ain't* right. They got *blood-wet* appetites for coloreds. Thanking you kindly for supper, but I must get on." She tries to stand but again collapses.

"It is your feet, honey," Ezra says, as he reaches into his satchel. "I am a doctor."

Bewildered, she stares at Ezra, not sure if she heard him right.

"A colored doctor?"

"Oh yeah," I say as I raise my footless leg. "The best. He will get you fixed up just right."

"No, not my feet! Please, Mister!" she cries. Ezra smiles as he retrieves a handkerchief and some whiskey.

"No, honey, just some bandages. It looks like you have some nasty cuts is all. I might need to sew one or two, but nothing *that* serious."

She is relieved, and then points to my missing foot. "What happened?"

"He shot me," I say.

"Why?"

"I probably deserved it." Ezra quietly gathers his

instruments as I have my fun.

He rolls out a blanket for her and asks that she lie down upon it with her feet close to the fire. He examines them and sighs.

"Seems some of these are worse than I thought." She struggles as he presses his fingers against some of the wounds. "No need to worry, dear. I have you now." She cries out as he pours a swallow's worth of whiskey over her feet, but she seems to know that it is for the best and tries not to squirm too much.

"Ezra, remind me to worry if you tell me not to," I quip, but he is undeterred and continues with his work. A few minutes later she is stitched up and settles along the blanket the best she is able. Her chains clank against each other as she wipes her teary eyes with both hands.

"Oh yes, those," Ezra says. "Would you like me to try to separate them?"

"Please," she says, as she wipes more tears from her face. Her feet must be on fire.

"Alse, you did much better than me," I say. Her lips curve into a tearful, incredulous smile.

Ezra bends down in front of her with two hunting knives. "Give me your wrists." She does. He places the points between one of the chain links and slowly pulls one of the knives toward him and the other away from him. After resetting the blades within the link several times he is able to break the bond and bend the link so that the adjacent loop slips out of the other. She pulls her wrists apart and smiles as wide as the night sky. "Tomorrow in the light I will see if I can get the cuffs around your wrists off as well."

"Thank you," she says as she continues to stretch her arms out to either side. After a moment her countenance returns to darkness. "I was running because Mama told me to run and do not stop running until nightfall. Mama told me that Master got a right price for me. That they was going to brand my face and take me away from her. That is why they chained me. But Mama helped me escape. So I done what Mama told me, and I ran."

"You can stay with us as long as you need," I say.

"Thank you, but they will be after me. I mean, they is after me." Tears spill down her cheeks. "I am sure when Master found out that I was not there, well, I am sure Mama had an awful whippin'."

"We will keep you safe. No need to fret over this now," Ezra says. "Now curl up with that blanket and get some rest. We will sort this out in the waking hours. Besides, you are not going anywhere with those feet."

About a half hour later I can hear only the hush of the woods and Ezra's steady snore. Slowly I begin to drift as Cora's song sings me into a dream.

February 1855
Eli, Age 18

This is not right. Cora looks into my eyes as we seem to float together. We are dancing in my father's home. A beautiful dress hangs upon her shoulders and beyond her feet. I am dapper and agile as I lead our dance.

I am healthy. I am strong. I can feel the powerful thrusts of my legs as I step with her. This is our wedding night. But something is amiss. I can feel it. Nobody is here with us. There should be people. Missus Hannah, my father . . . but no one. In fact, I cannot hear my steps. No music can be heard, and for that matter, I cannot hear the voice of my love as I watch her lips move.

I stop dancing. I feel her pull away from me as her expression twists into puzzlement, and then fright. My body weakens, as my dapper suit swells four sizes beyond the length of my bones. I reach for my face; my skin is pulled taut again, and my hands and arms are but bones covered in sickly flesh. I feel a molar loosen, and then another and another until the upper right side of my mouth spits into my waiting hands. Cora collapses to the floor with her back against the sofa. I feel my balance wane as my left foot withers to nothing. I reach for the top of a chair to my right, but discover I am too weak to stand. I fall within this oversized suit to the floor where we once danced with such elegance. And as I lie, I gaze upon my love. I can hear her now as she wails at the horror that has become her husband.

CHAPTER TWENTY-EIGHT

September 1863
Eli, Age 26

I jolt forward with Cora's anguish still shadowing my mind. But this is not why I woke. Something here is pulling me back into these woods. I hear a snap of a twig, and then a scuttle of footsteps. I am alert. The moon is near full and casts enough light for me to peer around camp. Alse is awake. I did not think she would have dozed easily. The whites of her eyes cut through the relative darkness as I stare into them. No doubt the encroaching footsteps are intended for our supper guest. I poke Ezra with my staff. I see his eyes open. He is quiet as he studies the coldness of my disposition. I hear a few more twigs crack under foot. Whoever they are, they are no longer running but scouting. Alse trembles under her blanket. I hear her shackles clink.

Two menacing growls try our nerves. A young man, maybe twenty, holds a rope tethered to a pair of unfriendly dogs. Beside him a man old enough to be his father wields a pistol. Ezra and I had drawn our guns long before the beasts wandered into our camp.

"Silence your dogs unless you wish me to restrain them," I say as I raise my revolver higher.

The one holding the rope commands the dogs in a harsh tongue, and they promptly sit. The older man locks eyes with Alse, but she is quick to cover her face with her blanket.

"Sorry to have alarmed you," he says, "but we are here to retrieve my property." He points the talking end of his pistol at the terrified lump of blanket.

"'Fraid I cannot let you do that," Ezra says with squinted eyes.

"Watch your lip, boy," the man snaps. "Ain't nobody speaking to you! This is white man's business. You have nothing to say about that little wench." He redirects his glower at me. For a moment I think Ezra is going to shoot him dead.

"Wench?" I say. "Your words seem misplaced. What has she done?" I ask.

"What has any colored done?" he scoffs. "I am here to retrieve my property—"

"If I kindly refuse?" I say.

"Young man," he says to me, "it looks as though that Colt is weighing down that sickly wrist of yours. Reckon you are not much up for a shootin'. I would prefer to leave here peaceably, but if we cannot reason, I may have to shoot you, cut the tongue out of this here chatty colored, and take him for all my troubles. Or maybe I will just shoot him dead and be done with it. Do you want to chance blood spilt over some worthless Negress?"

I sigh heavily. "She hardly seems worthless—with you tracking her in the devil's hour." I study the dogs and the young man. I *am* sick and with such an encumbrance I concede to myself that I am not nearly as fast as I used to be. "But you are right," I continue, "I do not wish to leave this world tonight and truly I would not appreciate losing my property much either." I look at Ezra. "Okay, take the girl."

She yelps.

The man grabs her by the arm, yanking her upward. She grimaces and falls to the ground hampered by the pain as she grabs for her tender feet. Her eyes are ablaze, as if she might tear my throat out if fate gave her such an opportunity. I turn to Ezra again. He is calm and silent.

"I just want a good night's sleep. Keep her quiet on the way out," I say. They head south, and as they leave I hear Alse's tearful song of betrayal. I load my Enfield and hand it to Ezra. "Wait a couple minutes."

He nods. I poke at the fire with my staff as I hear Ezra head east with a rifle in each hand and his pistol on his hip. About two minutes later, the crack of my rifle echoes through the trees, and three seconds after, I hear his rifle fire. But then the quiet returns and I am left with only my thoughts, and the night, and the moonlight showering above.

Ezra returns with a rattled girl in his arms. As he sets

her down on her blanket, he wipes tears from her face.

"Alse, you are safe now," he says. She seems grateful, but clearly distressed by Ezra's actions, as she does not speak a word.

Ezra hands me my rifle. I load it for another round with no plans of using it any time soon.

"The dogs?" I ask.

"They are busy devouring duck carcass," he says with a shimmer of offense. "I may be a sinful murderer . . . but I am not heartless. Now if you will pardon me, I have soil to turn." He unties a spade shovel from his saddle.

"A little late for gardening?" I ask with a chuckle.

But this night he does not share my humor.

CHAPTER TWENTY-NINE

October 1863
Eli, Age 26

A s our horses trot up to my father's home, I am thrown into boyhood memories that feel as real as the reins in my hands. For a moment I swear I witness a little boy and girl hand in hand scramble down the porch steps, but before I can utter a word they disappear before me. I am left staring at nothing more than weather-worn steps.

Ezra gently nudges Alse's arms under his as she hugs his back. She had fallen asleep miles ago. This nudge and the slowing cadence of Dottie's trot bring her about. Ezra dismounts Dottie and guides Alse from the saddle. We had bartered a pair of worn girl's shoes some days ago for which she was grateful. However, with her feet healing, she still cannot absorb the full impact of dismounting a horse.

It seems Alse has taken to Ezra. I think he has found himself a little sister. Ezra has promised that once I am settled they will go back to her plantation, and seek her mother and any others they could manage. To what end I do not know. In another life perhaps it is an adventure I could be a part of, but it seems my days are fated to be with my father and Missus Hannah. Truly I welcome the long restful days ahead of me.

Ezra loops the reins around a hitching post as he retrieves me from Freckles. He is mindful not to strip me entirely of my dignity as he allows me to maintain my weight against the stirrup, and then patiently waits as I swing my amputated leg over the horse's rump. I reach an arm around his massive neck, and he carefully lowers my body to the earth. Just as my foot touches the ground, I hear my father's boots knock against the porch. As Ezra hands me my staff, I release my hand from him.

My father's face is thinner, and his beard is speckled with white and silver. His forehead is cut deep with age. I doubt that he will be able to recognize me. I receive a timid half wave, his mouth slightly agape as he examines what has become of his only son. His eyes shift to Ezra and soften.

I hear the familiar scrape of the front door and am relieved and frankly delighted to see Missus Hannah drying her wet hands on a dishcloth. Her smile warms me from within, but as she absorbs the vision that has become of me, a hand rises to her heart, and she represses a gasp of shock.

Even with my downturn these last few days, I felt I was doing all right, but after such a sobering reception, I fear I may have been swept away in delusion. I am sick. I have been for a long time. This acceptance fills me with profound sadness because I know that I am going to die.

I press my staff into the soil. It sinks about five inches. To hold my balance better, I wedge it not only under my arm, but against my hip as well.

Ezra and Alse trot up the porch steps. It is really quite lovely to see Ezra and my father side by side.

"This is Alse," Ezra says. Missus Hannah smiles and takes the child by the hand. I have forgotten how much Missus Hannah and her daughter look alike. The warmth that I had felt just earlier has fallen away, and in the presence of this mother's smile I feel a beautiful weakness wash through me.

My father introduces himself to Alse, and then firmly embraces Ezra's waiting hand. "You are safe here," my father says to him.

"Some help here?" I laugh as I teeter uncomfortably. "I will not be able to hold on much longer. The soil, Ezra . . ." He jogs down the steps, and within a moment, one of his arms crosses my back, and his hand firmly holds my waist. He carries me as if it were only himself ascending the stairs.

My staff slides along the porch, but then halts in a knot as Ezra releases me. My father is silent. The sadness in his eyes reminds me of some of the harder days of being a boy in his keep.

"What has the war done to my son?"

"Papa," I say, "I fell apart long ago before the war." There is so much pain in his eyes. I feel a hesitant, but hardy hug embrace my bones. He pulls away from me with a compassionate smile, while lightly placing his palms against my shoulders. "Good to see you too, Papa."

"You hungry?" he says.

"Is a frog's arse watertight?"

"Boy, I do not rightly know."

"Father, I am hungry, famished, in fact."

I am guided into the parlor, and the smell of my childhood meets my nose. Not much has changed. The furnishings are in the right place, and most of my childhood whatnots are where I left them. The scent of root soup lifts my spirits as we move toward the kitchen. Alse is halfway into her bowl as Missus Hannah sets a small basket of bread next to her.

Missus Hannah seats me, and soon, I am spoon deep in soup with my fingertips soaking a piece of bread. Ezra and my father embrace again in the keeping room. I cannot hear what they are discussing, but it is solemn and between them. Perhaps it is about Ezra's adventures out west.

Soon, all of us surround the table. I share a broken smile—Ezra's dental work shining through—with my father, as his hand covers that of Missus Hannah.

She nestles her cheek against his shoulder, and I feel my soul settle as I absorb my father's new life. He is happy. They are happy.

"Ezra," I say, "are you still true to your promise?"

"Whenever you are ready," he says.

"An hour after first light then."

"What is happening in the morning?" Missus Hannah

asks.

"These two," Father says, "are going to pay their respects to Samantha."

"Oh, I will accompany them," she says.

"No, dear, it will be only Eli and Ezra this time." My father nods toward Ezra.

I wonder how he knows, but then it comes back to me. He has lived a similar fate. Perhaps he thinks the only reason why Ezra shall accompany me at all is that I could not possibly make the trip on my own.

"Who is Samantha?" Alse asks, as she pauses between slurps of soup.

"Someone I wish you could have met," I say.

Ezra holds my side as I lower myself to my knees. He places the staff alongside of me as my fingertips trace the engravings.

1837–1855
Here lies
Cora Samantha Hannah–West
Sister
Daughter
Wife
Mother

"The horses need rest. If you need me I will be at the brook just there." He points about a hundred yards away.

I nod, remembering splashing in it as a carefree boy so long ago. I feel his palm leave my shoulder. Moments later, I am alone with only the hush of Scarlet Maple leaves tussling above.

"I am not angry, not anymore," I say to the granite stone. It feels cold and unforgiving. Certainly not befitting such a warm soul. "Mostly I am confused. I am hurt. Bleeding from a wound that refuses to heal, no matter the secondhand remedy. I have been without your touch, without your smell, without your kiss for eight years. How I long.

"I have forgotten nothing. Not the way you shivered when I kissed your neck, or the way you laughed when I was a fool, nor your gaze when we made love.

"I wonder about our baby. If she is with you. If she is, in fact, a girl. You told me while in the joys of your pregnancy that our baby was to be a girl, and her name would be Amelia. She would be nearly eight now."

I look toward the sun as a breeze dwindles almost to nothing. The golden light washes over me as I close my eyes to the heavenly sky.

It is not the crack of the enemy Enfield rifle round that startles me. It is the sifting whispers of the bullet as it splits the wild grass in my direction.

Bone, blood, and fabric explode from my chest. My eyes widen as my hands clutch my sternum. I try to catch myself while reaching for her headstone. I smear blood across the top and down the face of her engraving as I collapse to my side. The earth is wet as it soils my face. My breath quickens. It is only now that I feel the shot through my back and out my chest. Redness surrounds me. But not death.

As I lie along her grave the morning light brightens, and before me Cora appears—an angelic figure mirroring me. Her cheek presses the earth as she lies with me. Her golden hair gently blows in the celestial air. The beauty of her gaze brings me to tears as I extend my bloody hand toward her for one last touch. She smiles calmly like she has been expecting me. She is filled with light. As our hands meet I feel peace come over me. No more sadness, no more loss. But yet I weep. She does too.

"Come back to me," I whisper as I lie against God's earth.

"I am here, I never left," escapes her wistful lips. "Come with me, my love. We have been waiting for you."

We stand together, my body now like hers, blissful and healed in God's grace. She pulls me gently. And as I begin to walk, before us I see Emily with a little girl by her side. "Amelia," I say. She hugs me, and as I scoop her up, in an instant her love overwhelms me.

I look back to find Ezra running toward my hemorrhaging body. His Enfield rifle exhales smoke as he collapses next to me. I lovingly watch as he casts his rifle aside and gently pulls his friend to his breast.

"Please forgive me, Eli. Forgive me . . ." he sobs.

For months my bones were sick through and through. I have known my plight. Death's beckoning finger has been rapping my shoulder for more days than I care to think about.

But in my death I am not sorrowed. I am thankful to have had such a friend in Ezra. I will never forget the gift he has given me and the sacrifice he must now carry in his heart. I hope one day to thank him for his selflessness. I wish I could tell him I am no longer hurting, that truly, I have found my peace.

As Cora holds my hand I feel her brush against me, and as I gaze upon her, I know that I am leaving this world, but at this end, instead of falling alone into the darkness—together, we fall into the light.

MALAIKA

VAN HEERLING

To date this novella has been downloaded more than 60,000 times.

THANK YOU, READERS.

Here is what people are saying about MALAIKA.

"BEAUTIFUL & HAUNTING..."

"Outstanding!"

"Immense and breathtaking."

"Hauntingly moving."

"Profound, thought-provoking, haunting."

"Simply stunning."

"Stunningly Beautiful."

"Wonderful, haunting & compelling."

"Captivating."

"Excruciatingly beautiful."

"Magical."

"An Extraordinary Story."

"An incredibly touching story!!!"

"This is why we read."

FREE CHAPTERS FROM MALAIKA

(Ma-lie-ka)

The first time I saw her, I was dazed but recovering from hellish nightmares. Not sure if it was the scent of coffee lackadaisically meandering across the Serengeti that brought us to our serendipitous moment (do big cats drink coffee?), or if it was that she had told me she'd be here soon. I generally don't have conversations with animals—other than the human kind. I suppose, if the dialogue occurred in a dream, you aren't crazy, right?

As far as how I came to live just inside Kenya at the Tanzanian border overlooking the Serengeti, well, that is another lifetime dappled with hurt and a lost love elsewhere in the world—I won't bore you with the details. I wanted to get as far away from that pain as I could. The 'geti is about as distant as I could travel. Funny, no matter how far one has traveled, the past is just a moment. . . just a thought away.

I will not taint this story with that past. This is a story of a more recent past, of a friendship—the most important friendship I've ever had.

I live east of a village. I am the only white man for probably twenty miles or more. I suppose there could be a few around, or many in town, but I haven't seen any. This life can be hard to adapt to, especially when one is accustomed to the rote American life of excess for its own sake. Pressure. That is part of the reason why I left. No, that is a lie. It's not why I left, but I promised I wouldn't scar this story with my American past. There may be a trace of it betrayed here and there, but I will do my best to check such impulses.

Where was I? Oh, yes—life is slower here. Not in a dim-witted way, but in a take-a-deep-breath-and-*live* kind of way. Speaking of breaths, I promised that I wouldn't start smoking again. But that was in my old life. I made a lot of promises then; this is now. I don't smoke processed cigarettes—Western market contraband. No, my good friend Abasi is a tobacco farmer. Did I say he's a good friend? He's a great friend; genuine, forthright, and not afraid to smack the hell out of you when you need it or deserve it. More often than not, I am the latter. Who would have known I'd have to travel halfway around the world to find a friend that wasn't a sycophant. One of his virtues is that he doesn't know the meaning of the word.

I teach Absko, his son, English in exchange for fresh tobacco, among other things. Truth told, I'd do it for free. He knows this. Sometimes I work the fields with him. Wielding a machete and tying bundles have been unbearably taxing at times. Although I have tried not to let it show on my face, everyone knows—I'm not fooling anyone. One could say I'm paying for my deep-seated American complacency, I suppose.

I must make one point very clear: I am not "anti-American way." Far from it. This is, like I said, just a different way of life. It is nothing here to slaughter your own food, or dig your own latrine, or hear of children starving to death, despite Doctors Without Borders. Unsheltered is what I mean. Far from texting and live streaming with friends.

I will one day go back. Maybe.

CHAPTER ONE

The weight of my waking body sagged as my hand dangled off the beaten plastic armrest. My fingertips stuck to the lip of an American coffee cup. Mostly because of the moisture in my palm, rather than my grip. My God, she was quiet. Had I been her culinary desire, I definitely would have been it. For some reason, the nostalgic disco beats of the seventies circled the air ducts of my mind. In hindsight, perhaps this was a coping mechanism. It seemed I had been through more in the last couple years than I cared to think about.

My other hand gingerly held a loosely rolled cigarette—in the early mornings I am not as motivated as most of the workforce, no doubt readying themselves for their day's toil.

I rolled the tobacco up to my lip, my eyelids shut to the cresting sun over Kenyan mountains. The fiery smoke warmed my throat from the morning chill. This African tobacco chars more tender throats, but my once-virginal uvula and esophagus had toughened up long ago. The fire these days simply continued to callous the linings of my ever-embattled breathing pipe. It's an acquired taste. It is earned, I suppose. An argument for my ex-wife? Perhaps.

It was to be a very clear day. January usually is, and hot of course. But this goes without saying—I wasn't used to the opposite seasons yet. The only ones who complain about the heat are foreigners, so I complain—God, do I complain.

I readjusted my back for a moment, lifting the slipping cup of joe to my mouth, and then lowering it back to its roosting spot a foot or so off the ground, dangling from my fingertips.

She was quiet. When you live in the wild and your hand is pushed into the air by what can only be bad, you notice. You notice real fast. I wasn't sure if I had leapt from the foldout chair when I heard the guttural sniff or if I was already standing. This was a beast. At least three hundred pounds—a big cat. She paid little attention to me at first. Sniffing the spilt coffee as it contoured to the cracked earth. Pawing it, she sniffed and lapped up what she could find. Then, licking her chops, she raised her head squarely at me. The sun looming over the mountains reflected in her eyes. Her body language was uninhibited, relaxed even, but those eyes—burned fierce.

Swiftly I realized that neither one of us was moving. Not good. I had frozen five feet away from her with my cigarette hand extended toward her as if the fiery cherry were a shield. I didn't want to be the first to move. Then, I remembered the "deer in the headlights" syndrome, and thought—shit, move your ass! Just as I was about to shift my body weight backward, her eyes flickered toward my intended route. Smart. They're not known as killing machines because they were guessers.

Lions never hunt alone . . . I was a goner for sure. Knowing this could be the end, I figured I better take another drag. When Abasi finds what was left of me, he'd discover the last remnants of his sweet, sweet tobacco. I gently pulled my cherry shield back to my lips. I wasn't dead yet or being dragged into the jungle. Good sign. So I sucked. It was the best smoke I'd ever had. Still not dead. Even better. I exhaled quietly as the smoke billowed from my mouth. She tilted her head up toward the expanding cloud of "Kenyan's Best," and, sniffing the air, her nostrils flared. She shook her head and huffed from the foreign and relatively concentrated dose.

Not that I wanted to see my disembowelment chasing me up, I did look, albeit slowly, to my right and my left. No other interested visitors that I could see. I wasn't about to turn my back on this feline. Although I was sure I'd be dead in less than five minutes, I gazed toward the house. It was wide open, both doors and all three windows. Even if I could manage to get inside, she'd be on my heels or through a window before I could grab and cock my shotgun. I'd be wrestling a full-grown lion in a four hundred square foot sand brick hut. That is, if I could even make it through the door.

She never took her eyes from me as she sniffed the air again. I billowed out yet another tobacco cloud. She sniffed the air a third time, but didn't recoil from the smoke. Placing one paw toward me, her eyes continued to deadlock on mine but they now lacked the fierceness of before. She sniffed the air again, I puffed again, and she took another step toward me. Too close. I panicked and feebly pushed the cigarette from my hand. It landed just in front of her fuchsia and ebony-edged nostrils. I took two steps back. She noticed, but preoccupied herself with my token expression of "please-don't-eat-me." Huddling in front of the smoldering tobacco, hunched down, she investigated the curious object.

"Careful. It's h—" Her tongue peeled from her massive mouth and pressed against the ember. She yelped loudly and hissed, bouncing backward. "—ot," I finished. She shook her head angrily in my direction, as if to say, "How about a little warning next time?"

"I tried to tell you but—" That was when I realized I was talking to a lion. I'm not sure why, but she didn't eat me. Her composure came back somewhat as she began to cautiously pull her body forward. She was proud. Head high, shoulders and back straight. Really just a marvelous creature. The muddled russet coat was truly brilliant to behold, especially so close up.

I held my hand out palm up because I'm an idiot, I know… but it seemed like the proper thing to do at the time. I was right. She tentatively pressed the crown of her head against my knuckles. I wasn't ready for the sheer power. She rubbed her body against my pant leg, nearly knocking me to the ground. I pressed my hand against her fur. It was surprisingly soft, but thick and rugged—if it is possible to be both at the same time. She circled me two times. I didn't move much. Then, she treaded her footsteps back to my chair, sniffed at the coffee-sodden ground again, and trotted back into the jungle.

I felt ashamed about wanting to take her down. Although I'm sure it crossed her mind once or twice. So maybe we were even.

CHAPTER TWO

By the time Absko showed up, it was late morning, coming upon noon. He was a strong boy. His body well into the advanced stage of puberty; that awkward period when you're not sure which or what was growing. He approached shirtless. It wasn't hot for him and truth be told, vanity was setting in these days. His upper body could now bear two heavy bundles of tobacco with little effort.

My door was always open, more or less. It wasn't like I had a dead bolt or anything, or even a lock. Anyone coming out this far would be intending to see me, and I haven't as of yet, made any enemies that I knew of.

The screen door yielded its familiar whine as the coiled metal spring flexed—subsequently slapping the door shut as Absko entered. He set his books on a small table accompanying a worn book of Emerson, headed for the icebox, and popped open an A&W. I had just gotten them. My favorite.

"Absko," I said, "what did you learn today?"

"At school or in life?" he replied, anticipating my answer.

"In life, my boy, in life!" This was routine talk between us; somehow, it hadn't run its lot yet.

"I learned today that I could lie to my father and get away with it." He waited, testing me to see if I'd approve or rebuke such a discovery.

"Hmm, I see. Yes, very good—learning the art of

deception. However, don't be surprised if that comes back to haunt you one day. Especially if your father never finds out."

"Don't you want to know what it is about?"

"And there it starts . . . nope, Absko, I most definitely do not want to know about it. That is yours alone."

"What 'starts'?" he questioned.

"You'll find out soon enough. I'll give you a hint, though. Deception is a wicked instrument, and when used against the ones we love . . . well, like I said, you'll one day learn a new lesson."

"Are you going to tell him?"

"No, Absko, but you might."

He took a sip of root beer as he brooded over this. As a bright boy, I knew he basically understood my warning, but the full circle of understanding wouldn't hit him until life pressed it on him.

"Nah, I don't think he needs to know, not about this one."

I pulled a root beer for myself and traded a wry smile with him. Abasi was my best friend, but only if it were dire enough would I break the confidence I had earned from his son. I had a feeling Absko's deceit in this case was child's play (I was wrong).

I grabbed my tobacco pouch and some papers and headed to my dilapidated but trusty chair just out front. Absko followed silently, grabbing his yellow, faded foldout, and set up next to mine.

"So have *you* learned anything today?" he asked.

"Hmm, yes. I learned I might not be as safe out here as I thought I would be."

Absko raised his head from the back of his chair, a bit frightened. I had never spoken of such things. He waited for me to continue.

"I was visited by a lioness, 'bout three hundred pounds."

"Ha! OK, funny, you got me. You'd have been shredded." When I didn't reciprocate his playfulness, it sunk in. "A lioness? Are you serious?"

"Yep, gorgeous too. Check the paw prints at your feet." He did, his eyes wide open. "She knocked my coffee—"

"You didn't shoot it?"

"Oh no, first of all, I would have been done for had she so desired. Plus, the gun was in the house. But I have to tell you, she looked right at me. It was almost like she just came by to say hello."

"How many were there?

"Just her."

"No, that is what she wanted you to see. When they hunt, there would have easily been five or six stalking you."

"She wasn't hunting," I said plainly.

"How do you know?"

"Well, Absko, I'm talking to you, aren't I?"

He fell quiet. He didn't like what I was saying. No one was a friend of the felines. Most of the time the cats were killed on sight if they entered the villages. Most probably knew not to enter, and the ones that didn't know usually learned with their lives. Absko's cousin was killed by one of them. An all-out hunt was summarily dispatched against the nearest pride. Perhaps the saddest thing besides the loss of his cousin was that no one was sure if the particular pride they slaughtered was the offending family. No matter, of course, to men of revenge and reckoning.

"Well, I don't like it. Have you told my dad?"

"You're the first person I have seen today. When you see him, ask him to bring some of the passion fruit and bobby beans he had last week. I'm all out."

"No problem. You should lock your door tonight."

"Don't have a lock. I'll be all right. Like I said, it was just the one. Hey, Absko, let's keep this between us for the time being."

"Sure. I learned another thing today."

"Yeah? What's that?"

"I think I'm going to need a new English teacher," he said, straight-faced.

"Well, it wouldn't be the first time I've been dominated by a pussy," I retorted. It was immature I know, but I knew it'd get a rise out of a sixteen-year-old. "Cheers," I chuckled, as we clanked tin cans together and drank the sweet nectar they call the "Beer of Root."

CHAPTER THREE

I slept fully, unlike most nights. And unlike most nights, I dreamed. I preferred nothingness while sleeping in place of the nightmares, of course. But up until last night, I had nearly forgotten the pleasures of dreams without horrifying qualities. She came back to me. We sat next to each other and watched the sunrise. I put my hand on her back and petted her golden coat—speckled with a rusty brown and slivers of ebony. And for some reason, to my right lay my wife on her own foldout chair. She was young like when we first met, sunbathing, rubbing oil on her arms and neck. Smiling at me like nothing had happened. She was happy. Then I woke up. The sun would show soon.

As before, I held my coffee at the tips of my fingers. I half-hoped, crazy as it might seem, that she would come back and that the dream would be more than a random projection of my own desires. Sipping my coffee, I trembled at the thought of her, the cat, coming back—not my wife. Two different creatures altogether. The cat could disembowel me, after all—well, now that I think of it, the ex could, too.

The foldout chair creaked and twanged under my weight. The peeking sun was just beginning to caress the mountaintops. I took another sip as the golden light splashed across my face. If not for the overpowering taste of the coffee, I could have smelled this light. I looked to my right and saw not a sun-tanning twenty-five-year-old other half, but an empty meadow, flush with wild grasses, the tips of which were painted by the light—kissing them with auburn and blond hues.

To my left was a cat staring into the rising sun with such concentration, I thought she might be praying to a light god. Perhaps, if I had any good sense, I would have recreated the same spectacle as yesterday: the dramatic leap from the thrifty foldout with my arms pressed forward while hiding behind the cherry glow of my loosely rolled cigarette. For starters, I don't have any sense, and also, I had yet to prep a smoke. Instead, I sat. I sat with my legs stretched across the length of the plastic chair, my boney kneecaps exposed to a potential mauling.

Who am I kidding? My whole body could be a chew toy to her. I raised my coffee to my bottom lip. The steam effervesced against my face as I swallowed. She had a glint of green within her eyes that I hadn't noticed before. I noticed this after the sound of my sip pulled her from her prayer to the sun god. She was unpretentious as she stared directly into my eyes. I wasn't sure what to do, so I smiled gently, making sure not to expose my teeth just in case it be construed as universal aggression. Her attention did not go to my mouth, but rather stayed with my eyes. I swear my smile was reciprocated, as she then maneuvered her head back to the shimmering light splintering over the mountains.

Déjà vu struck me as I turned my gaze to the mountains as well. This was my dream. I looked to my right, again expecting to see my wife, but of course, she wasn't there. My friend turned to me again, seemingly acknowledging my thought. Slowly I reached for my tin full of tobacco and papers. My lioness friend was not threatened by me. And to my surprise, my guard had been slipping away. She pouted her nose in the air toward the tin just as she'd done before when she smelled the tobacco smoke the first time.

"Oh, you remember this, don't you?" I said, breaking the silence. My voice was thick. As I rolled a cigarette, she studied my process. Her eyes then lifted to my face as I lit it. A puff of white smoke expelled from me. Her nostrils flared delightfully as she moved closer, bumping the arm of the chair. I nearly toppled over. I let her smell it as I set it in front of her nose, my hand mere inches from her pink-stained mouth. Intrigued by this smell, she rolled her tongue out to lap it. Retracting my hand as fast as I could narrowly missing the rasp that was her tongue, I said, "No, hot!"

Her head tilted forward as she contemplated my sounds. She snorted annoyingly and sat back down on her haunches. I think she remembered the burning of her tongue on the previous ember. I took another drag and exhaled. She enjoyed it vicariously through me as the smell permeated the air around us. Then, because I'm stupid, remember, I placed my hand on her back. She allowed me to pet her a bit, and then she got up and began her return to the meadow. I didn't intend to follow her, but she stopped and waited for me. This was unfamiliar territory. The dream had come to fruition for the most part. She took me fifty yards from the perimeter of my property, further into the meadow. This was apparently the point where Tanzania and the actual Serengeti began. As far as I was concerned, it was all 'geti to me. Beyond the perimeter was a shallow valley hidden by a rim of trees and bush. Beyond that point, I no longer felt safe. When first settling in, I walked most of the area around my home. As I approached this area, I felt— tracked. From that point on I learned to stay on the trails that led to the village and water supply.

Standing next to me, her back at my waist, I soon realized why she stopped. At the tree line sat three cold-faced lions. A male in the middle and two lionesses. To say they were jovial to see us would be a funny twist of truth. Soon, my friend mirrored their unfriendly posturing. I stood there like an oaf.

No wonder I felt like I was being tracked when I had journeyed this way. For all intents and purposes, I probably was. But this time, this moment, was immeasurably worse. Was I breakfast? Had I been betrayed by my new friend? A tremor of terror struck me. She must have figured out what I was thinking because she flanked my leg and nuzzled my hand with her head. I felt better, but not confident I was going to walk away safe. Not a flinch from the audience of three. Her actions toward me had distilled their disapproval into more of a fury, and then they glowered.

Submissively, she bowed her head, tucking her tail in close to her legs as she walked the fifty yards to her—guardians? I raised my hand as she tentatively looked back at me before disappearing through the trees and down into the ravine. The females had followed her. As for me, the king of beasts stood squared to me not fifty yards from my boney knees. My gnawable, boney knees. He took one step forward. His entire coat shook as he stepped into a definite and calculated pose. No need for a lion-to-human translation. He did not scan the land around me. He did not flinch. His address was to me. A gentle breeze wisped through the king's mane. As if made of stone dressed with russet fur, he did not budge. Rock-solid. His chin rose and nostrils flared, just like my friend. But his was a malevolent gesture. He'd deciphered my scent. A scent he wouldn't soon forget. The roar that now came from his mouth was more of a guttural rebuke. I was an annoyance to him. Then, although moderated, the second roar seemed to concentrate within my inner ear and did not penetrate much further than the meadow. This warning was for me alone, not for the surrounding African audience. It was acute, painful.

Unknown to me, until I felt the warmth percolating through the fabric of my drawers, a splash of fright had wetted my leg. I was able to halt it, but couldn't make any promises if another step was taken. His scruff was pinkish with blood, similar to my visitor. Even if he may have already eaten, it didn't mean he wouldn't still feast upon the problem at hand. His belly was capacious, no doubt from several large meals in his lifetime. I'm sure half a zebra and an unclean washed-up schmuck could fit just fine, albeit snugly. On the other hand, he could simply maul me just to prove a point. Either way, I was at his mercy. Couldn't run to the house, and even if I could, I doubted the walls could hold a four-hundred-pound cat from a determined entrance.

Calculatingly, his shoulders commandeered his body back to the tree line, his man-lion parts swaggering from side to side. Then he was gone.

Soaking in my surroundings, I felt the high grass at my fingertips and heard White-tailed Swallows singing their songs. Up to this point, I had not known they were cheerfully crooning to their mates while my life, as seemingly inconsequential as it was, hung in the balance. Had the now-absentee king decided to tear me limb from limb, these cheery birds of the Serengeti might have improvised a lovely melody while I wailed and pleaded for my existence.

And there, two hundred yards from my own home, I peed myself. I peed myself uncontrollably.

GET YOUR COPY OF MALAIKA

ABOUT THE AUTHOR

For Van Heerling, writing is a therapy of sorts—a way to let go. Few things in life bring him such relief.

A native to California, Heerling now resides in the Pacific Northwest with his family, preferring the dreary sky to the sun scorching days of Southern California.

He enjoys hearing from readers. If you wish to send your comments, visit his website at:

www.vanheerlingbooks.com

Made in United States
North Haven, CT
12 July 2022

21228140R00102